WHAT ONCE WAS PERFECT

WARDHAM BOOK 2

ZOE YORK

ZOYO PRESS

COPYRIGHT

DEDICATION

from the past, for the future

In memory of my Mom, one of the original self-publishers, who taught me that I can do anything

For my sons, who are daily reminders of the primacy of love, and in memory of Lynda, who helped raise them

1

K yle Nixon grabbed the empty bowl of chips from his coffee table and kicked his brother's feet out of the way as he headed for the kitchen.

"That's no way to treat your guests, especially when they're the ones who provided the entertainment in the first place," Ian groused, but his grin belied any grumpiness. Kyle knew his older brother was just happy to have a rare afternoon for vegging out on the couch and playing the latest first-person shooter game. Ever since his daughter fell behind in her reading homework, Ian's wife Carrie had banned video games from their farmhouse.

As a teacher, Kyle understood.

As a gamer, though, he felt his brother's pain.

The obvious solution had been for Kyle to selflessly volunteer to house the brand new PlayStation at his own place. He was generous like that. It looked fan-fucking-tastic next to his Xbox.

A knock at the door interrupted his search through his pantry for more snacks. "Evan's here."

"He'll let himself in," Ian mumbled between shots fired.

He would. Kyle's half-renovated schoolhouse just outside of their small lakeside town had become the de facto bachelor hangout pad, even though Evan had just built a killer house on the bluffs overlooking his winery.

The Nixon and West brothers were now from two different worlds, but they were still the best of friends. Video games and beer had a way of bonding guys for life like that.

Before Kyle could holler that the door was open, Evan was inside, kicking the first snow of the year off his boots. "I'm moving to Hawaii."

"You'd miss us too much."

"They have people in bikinis and board shorts there, year round. You assholes don't compete with that kind of eye candy."

Kyle snorted. "Then go."

Evan growled something about too much work to do and threw himself onto the couch next to Ian. Two grumpy old men. They deserved each other as best friends.

He resumed his search for snacks. "I've got pretzels. Maybe we should order in some pizzas."

"Already on it," Evan said over his shoulder, his eyes not leaving the TV screen. "Ty's in the city. He's picking up dinner on his way here."

Kyle grabbed his phone and shot off a quick text that they needed more beer. It was shaping up to be that kind of afternoon.

The fucking awesome kind.

If his brother and best friends weren't there, he'd...what? Probably finish the trim along the far wall. Maybe get started on the framing off of his bedroom, which was currently just blocked off by a heavy curtain.

He liked carpentry, but it was a poor substitute for human company.

Time to start dating again. But the way things had ended with Crystal, he wanted to have his head on straight.

As long as his fingers twitched to type Laney Calhoun's name into the search bar on his Internet browser, he wasn't ready.

It had taken a Herculean effort not to stalk her online. He

knew she was in Chicago now. Five hour drive if traffic was kind. Just across the Canada-US border.

Laney Calhoun. Whip-smart, beautiful beyond measure. Hated his guts. Still owned a tiny bit of real estate on his heart and probably always would, because he was a fool.

He'd hurt her so badly she hadn't come back to Wardham for longer than a weekend visit in more than a decade.

And the only time they'd seen each other, in a crowded room at her father's funeral, he'd found himself at a loss for words.

He took a deep breath and shook it off. It was for the best that Crystal had left him. And it was for the best that he get over Laney and move on with his life.

He'd done it once. And now he was doing it again. He squeezed his hands on the edge of the granite countertop. He'd renovated this house up from an empty shell. Designed the kitchen himself. Installed a wood stove in the living room and hung a big screen TV, flanked on either side by bookshelves. It was warm and cozy and the best damn bachelor pad a geek could ever want.

Now he just needed to get his head back in the game and find a woman to drag back to his lair.

———

"Mr. Nixon!"

Kyle suppressed a grin as the eager ten-year-old hopped up and down in front of him. "Yes, Michaela?"

"Andrew's going to be late, but he has a good reason."

"Yeah?" He hovered his pen over the attendance sheet. "Did you see him this morning?"

She nodded, dancing back and forth on her feet. It was four days before the Christmas break. They were all a little antsy. "His mom is taking him to the grocery store to get some canned goods for the food drive."

And the hidden grin fell away. *Shit.* Andrew's mother worked two jobs and the last thing she needed to do was buy food to keep up with the Joneses. He hated the messages that the school sent home. Yes, it was important to collect donations for the food bank. But promising the kids that the class with the biggest donation pile would get a pizza lunch on the last day of school before the break…

He gritted his teeth and gave Michaela a smile. "Thanks. I'll hold off on ten minutes before sending this down." Andrew didn't need another late recorded on his file, either. He cleared his throat and lifted his voice. "Does everyone have their planner out? Good. As soon as the announcements and anthem are over, please write down these three notes for your parents to read." He pointed at the smart board. "And once you've got that done, find your free reading book for the week. I want everyone to have at least one chapter read before we move on to the science lesson."

As the intercom squawked to life, the door flung open and Andrew hurried through. Kyle gave him a welcoming wave and marked him as present. "And who wants to take the attendance down to the office?"

––––––––

AT THE END of the day, he straightened up his classroom and finished his notes on the reading assessments he'd done on two students that day. One was just fine, but the other was falling behind. He'd bring it up with the reading resource teacher the next day, but tonight he had something just as important to do.

He drove the few blocks from the school to Wardham's main drag and parked in front of his sister-in-law's bakery. He'd grab some coffee and muffins once he'd done this one little good deed.

At least he hoped it was a good idea.

Karen Miller wouldn't hesitate to tell him if he was on the wrong track. And she'd keep his secret if it was a good plan.

He found her in the back office at Wardham Grocery, and

knocked on the open door. She glanced up from her computer. "Hey."

Karen had been a year between Ian and Kyle at school, and he'd always liked her. *Date this one*, his brain said. She was pretty and smart and kind, and just as much a homebody as Kyle was. Karen would never leave Wardham. She wasn't destined for Harvard and a big-city career as a surgeon.

But his heart didn't leap at the warm, welcoming smile on the other side of the desk. And in the thirty years they'd known each other, not once had she ever shown any interest in him beyond board game nights and trading library book recommendations back and forth.

"Earth to Kyle…"

He laughed and shook his head. "Sorry. Long day."

She tilted her head to the side. "What's up?"

"I need a favour, and I'm treading close to the line in even talking about this with you, so I don't want you to ask me why and this has to stay between us."

Her eyebrows hit the roof. "Okay."

"For real."

"I only gossip about your dating life. Mum's the word if it's anything else."

"No worries on that front." He took a deep breath. "You pay pretty close attention to who's in the shop, right? Work the front cash sometimes, that kind of thing?"

She nodded. "Of course. For the gossip." She winked. "And other reasons."

"One of my students…I'd like his mother to win a gift card that I'll pay for. Tell her it's the person who shopped just before her, or she's the random hundredth shopper of the day, something like that."

"We rarely get a hundred shoppers in a single day."

"Week, then. You know what I mean."

Her eyes went soft and she dropped the teasing tone. "I do. Who's the student?"

He hesitated, then gave her Andrew's mother's full name.

Instantly, she was out of her chair and her arms were wrapped around his neck. "Kyle Nixon, you're a good fucking egg, you know that?"

He laughed and returned her hug. "Tell my mom that."

"I will. And then we'll find you a nice girl to settle down with."

"Nope, don't do that."

"Too late, already on it." She squeezed him tight, then stepped back. "Just tell me how much and consider it done. She's in here a few times a week."

"Thanks. I owe you one."

"Not at all. Happy to help. Tis the season, and all that."

2

L aney slid her laptop into her leather messenger bag and flicked off the overhead light in her office. She paused at her secretary's desk to steal a peppermint chocolate square and drop off a light blue jewelry box wrapped in a white ribbon. One of the perks of living and working in downtown Chicago—easy access to awesome shopping.

The tap and scratch of pen on paper sounded from across the hall and she hesitated. She could sneak out, but she wanted this resolved before the holidays. The affair with Rick had been a mistake from the beginning, they were on the same page about that, but how do you move back to just being friends and colleagues?

The door pushed open as she knocked, and Rick looked up from his desk. "You're off, then?"

"Yep. I just wanted to say...Merry Christmas."

"You sure I can't convince you to come to the lake house with me?"

She shook her head with a rueful smile. "Let's not do this again, Rick. I'm not the girl you should take home to meet your mom."

"I know. Woulda been convenient if you were." He returned

her bittersweet expression and gestured for her to take a seat. "Don't you ever want more, though?"

"I...I used to." She sagged into one of the two chairs across from him and scrubbed her face with her hands. Once upon a time, she'd wanted it all. "If I was capable of falling in love, you'd be the perfect guy."

"Shame that's not how it actually works."

She bit her lip and nodded, although it wasn't like she was an expert on healthy relationships. Quite the opposite. Laney had banned emotional entanglements from her life a long time ago. Never again would she be vulnerable and give her heart to someone. It wasn't worth the pain.

She barely did physical relationships, only agreeing to enter into a sexual arrangement if the interested party understood he would need to get tested and be monogamous for the duration. Condoms and birth control were mandatory. Most men cooled off in a hurry when they heard those terms. Rick had chuckled and scheduled a follow up discussion for a week later, when he presented her with a clean bill of health.

They joined DermaNorth at the same time a year earlier, both fresh out of plastic surgery residency programs, and she had seen him date two other women in the intervening months. Both relationships had been casual, brief and ended amicably, exactly what she liked. So they negotiated terms: Laney wanted an escort to fundraising events and didn't like overnight guests; Rick didn't want to leave in the middle of the night, but promised not to linger in the morning or expect breakfast.

"I'm sorry that I changed the rules on you."

Seriously, what kind of guy apologizes after a woman breaks up with him? Laney hated herself a little bit for not being open to exploring something more with Rick. But while their time together had been nice, that's all it had been. Physical compatibility and pleasant conversation. "What happened? Is it the holidays? More pressure from your parents?"

"Honestly? I think it was my birthday. Another year older, and what do I have to show for it?"

Laney cocked her eyebrow in disbelief. "Your career?"

"There's gotta be more to life than this, Laney." His lips quirked, then he cleared his throat. "Well, for us mere mortals, anyway."

"Hey! I have a life outside work." She paused, then dipped her head, acknowledging the point. "Okay, I don't, but—"

He interrupted her with a chuckle and she feigned a glower before continuing. "I get it, I really do. You want someone to come home to at the end of the day, even if it's in the middle of the night and all they do is rub your back for a minute after you stumble to bed. Someone who knows that when you scratch your nose at family dinners, it means you need to be rescued. Someone who can read your moods and bring you wine or chocolate or run you a bath without being asked. You're ready for sweatpants and watching TV on the couch, and loving every minute of it."

He stared at her, and she realized her voice had drifted to a whisper. "Holy shit."

"What?"

"Laney Calhoun, you've been in love before."

"Shut up."

"Tell me about him." He leaned forward, propped his elbows on the desk, and steepled his fingers. The wicked gleam in his eyes was annoying, but at least she didn't need to worry about leaving a broken heart behind over the holidays.

"Never going to happen." She pushed herself to a stand. "It's late, I have to go."

"Hey." Rick raised his hands, as if stop her, then dropped them to his desk. "Have a safe trip."

———

She inched her car forward. She'd made it to Detroit without hitting much traffic, but there was always a bit of a line at the border. Bright lights flooded the concrete area around the toll booths, obscuring the rise of the Ambassador Bridge against the early dawn sky. She counted the coins she needed again, knowing she had the right amount but indulging her obsessive nature because no one was there to make fun of her. As the truck in front eased past the toll booth onto the bridge, she rolled down her window. This routine was familiar, if not comfortable. Heading home always stirred up conflicting emotions. On the other side of the bridge lay the university. She could already feel the pang of regret that would lance through her gut as she drove past, an unavoidable reaction to a place so tied up in her memories of Kyle. The library. Their favourite Italian restaurant just off-campus. A few blocks further, and she'd pass his first apartment. It would have been her first home away from the farm if things had worked out differently.

She'd only seen him once in the last decade, at her father's funeral two years earlier. A decade had hardened her heart enough that she was able to shake his hand and ignore the liquid warmth that slithered up her arm. Able to hear his words of condolences and pretend they wouldn't ring in her ears for hours after. He stood in front of her in the church basement for a few extra moments, the line of community members paused behind him, and for a moment she thought he would say something else, but then he shook his head and moved on to give her mother a quick hug and repeat the same generic platitudes. By the time the receiving line had dwindled, he was gone. It was for the best, she had reminded herself at the time. No point in picking at old wounds. She'd learned her lesson twelve years ago, the last summer she spent in Wardham, the first summer she'd allowed herself to have a fling. The only summer she'd spent in love.

The delay wasn't significant on the other side of the bridge. Within minutes, she had pulled up to the Canadian border crossing and was handing over her identification to the guard in the booth.

"Where are you from?"

"I'm a Canadian citizen living and working in Chicago."

"Do you have any alcohol or tobacco in the car?"

"One bottle of champagne."

"Anything else to declare?"

"No."

"Welcome home." The border guard passed back her passport and waved her on.

For better or worse, Laney thought.

Traffic thinned and the first rays of a winter sun appeared on the horizon. In her rearview mirror, Windsor and the United States behind it were still dark with night. On either side of the highway, drifts of snow spotted the fields. Lights flicked on in barns and farmhouses, and Laney kept her eyes peeled for suicidal deer as she passed the occasional stand of trees. Fifteen minutes down the highway, she took the bypass to the exit for Wardham, and despite her previous reservations, she smiled. Essex County would forever be home in her heart.

Three side roads zipped past before the home stretch. She knew this road well. The next farm belonged to the Frids, the one after that to the De Limas. The old school house on the corner had been an artist's retreat the last time she was home, but the sign was gone now. If she kept driving straight, she'd soon be in town, all six streets of it, then catch a first glimpse of Lake Erie. She used to love the town beach, calm water stretching out as far as the eye could see. As she did every time she visited, however, she turned left on Concession Road 2. She only came home to visit her family, and probably would stay at the farm until she left again for Chicago.

There, on top of a slight rise, was Evening Lane Farm. Her parents had liked to tell people that they'd named it after their daughters, but Laney and Evie knew it was the other way around. They didn't mind. The farm was beautiful, the long lane lined with oak trees leading to a gabled yellow brick house, the pastures to the east and west neatly squared off with white fence. A wide lawn stretched between the house and the two barns farther back, and the gravel drive continued past it, disappearing behind the larger barn, all the way to the bush. Her dad had loved taking them out on the wagon to choose a Christmas tree. Last year they'd picked one up at the grocery store in town. Last year, she'd only come home for two days.

The kitchen light was on already when she pulled her car to a stop beside the house. She grabbed her empty Starbucks travel mug and stepped into the frosty air.

"Delaney Calhoun, you must have driven all night!"

"Hey, Mom." She jogged to the open door and swept her mother into a big bear hug. "Look at you, you're practically disappearing on me."

Claire Calhoun blushed and patted her trim hips. "Evie has me doing Pilates five mornings a week. You're lucky today is a rest day."

"You look great." Laney hung her coat on her hook behind the kitchen door, labeled with crayon lettering her eight-year-old self had pressed into the wood, claiming that spot forever. "Coffee on?"

"Of course. Your sister and the boys will be down any minute. I thought I'd make eggs and bacon for breakfast, but Evie has a new protein pancake recipe she wants to try out instead."

Laney made a face. At least the coffee would be good.

"How's she doing, anyway?"

"Better than I am."

"I'd hope so. Her husband was a douchebag, Mom, and he didn't die. Big difference."

"I know, but there's still grief in divorce."

"They tell you that in group therapy?"

"How'd you know?" Claire smiled brightly. "I think they were also supposed to tell you that at medical school, smarty-pants."

Laney opened her mouth to point out that med school was actually quite a long time ago, and counselling wasn't a significant part of the curriculum anyway, but she was interrupted by what sounded like a stampede of elephants coming down the stairs.

"SLOW DOWN. Seriously, Connor, you're going to kill your brother. Max, don't push him."

As if they hadn't heard their mother, two very excited little boys slid into the kitchen on sock feet and bounced into the new arrival.

"Aunt Laney, Aunt Laney, you're here!"

"Did you bring us presents?"

"We're going to get a tree today!"

"Do you want to see a magic trick?"

"You can sleep in our room if you want."

"We've been really good, don't listen to mom."

Laney collapsed into a pile of excited chatter with two of her most favourite people and beamed up at her older sister. "Hey! So we're getting a tree today?"

Connor poked her in the shoulder. "Don't forget about the presents."

Evie hauled him off the floor with a gentle reminder that eight-year-old boys should mind their manners and set good examples for their little brothers by offering to help make breakfast before they start asking about presents.

"Would you like some cardboard pancakes, Aunt Laney?"

"Why yes, Connor, I would, thank you. I love cardboard." She winked at Evie. "No cheat days over the holidays, sis?"

"Maybe for Christmas morning. But you're here for ten days. If we ate crap that long, we wouldn't have any energy to tromp through the bush, or have snowball fights, would we guys?"

Max pulled on Laney's hand. She bent down and he whispered in her ear, "I don't mind the pancakes. Grandma lets us have as much maple syrup as we want."

"Good to know," she whispered back.

Max was right. With enough syrup, the pancakes made from egg whites, oats and cottage cheese didn't taste bad at all.

After breakfast, Laney cleared the table and ran the dishwasher. As she wiped down the counter, Evie came into the kitchen dressed in yoga pants and a long sleeve t-shirt with a puffy down vest over top. Her long blond hair was pulled into a high ponytail. They shared the same blue eyes and fair colouring, but Laney didn't see the faint lines on her older sister that she could feel on her own face. It might be time for Botox. "Where are you off to?"

"I have to run into town for a bit, I've got a group Pilates session at the studio and we're low on groceries. I'll show you the app I use on my phone, you can add stuff to the list before I get to the store."

"Multi-tasking mom, eh?"

Evie paused and grinned. "And loving every second of it. Little did I know that divorce would be the best thing that ever happened to me."

"I want to hear all about that later. What should I do while you're gone?"

"Convince the boys to get dressed? We'll go to the bush to get a tree when I get back."

Laney reached her hand out to rest on Evie's arm. "Is Mom going to be okay with that?"

"Of course! Her idea, actually. She's gone over to Ted's farm to pick up the wagon."

3

___

Laney was hiding under a blanket on the couch. It had taken her an hour to corral Connor and Max into their room, and after promising them chocolate from her secret stash, they had agreed to get dressed for the day. She hadn't meant to lie down, but after her long drive a little catnap sounded perfect. She could hear faint peals of laughter, then thumping, a door opening and next, more clearly this time, Max counting. Another game of hide-and-seek. Pounding steps told her Connor planned on hiding in the attic, and she closed her eyes.

Her moment of peace was soon interrupted, not by target-seeking little boys, but a knock at the back door. Pulling the afghan around her shoulders, she padded into the kitchen. Bright light poured in the windows from the mid-morning sun. A large male body that she would recognize anywhere filled the glass window in the door. Seeing him here, on her mother's doorstep, was both familiar and completely unexpected. Her steps faltered and she stopped a few feet shy of the door.

At the funeral, he had worn a suit, and looked handsome, clean-cut and grown-up, a very different man than the college student she had loved. On her mother's doorstep in a fitted ski jacket and a wool toque, he looked like...himself. Shoulders a bit broader, maybe, but his body still looked lean and hard, even disguised by winter layers. Sunlight caught half of his stubble-flecked jaw. She could feel the rasp of his cheek against hers.

She dragged in a ragged breath and pressed her palms to her side. Her pulse felt thready, and she wondered if she might pass out. Fight or flight? No, Laney would faint. She closed her eyes and willed herself to not see him as a threat. Their last encounter had been entirely reasonable. She'd been distracted by grief and they'd been surrounded by people, but this was the boy that broke her heart. *Man.* This was the man who broke her heart. Now here he was, on her doorstep, looking far too fine. And they were alone. She could faintly hear the boys upstairs, and hoped that they wouldn't notice the visitor.

Kyle didn't seem surprised that she hadn't opened the door. He ducked his head for a moment, as if acknowledging that this must be awkward, then lifted it again, his mouth set in a straight line.

"Hey," he mouthed, then turned and pointed at the driveway.

She edged closer, peering out the side window. A green tractor was parked beside her Audi, a large farm wagon hitched behind it. She stared at the tractor, wondering if the next few minutes of her life could maybe not happen. When Kyle didn't magically disappear, she took a deep breath and opened the door.

"Hi."

"Your mom asked me to drive the wagon over."

She raised her eyebrows in disbelief. "My mom."

"Yeah. Laney ... I didn't know you were here, she didn't say."

She stared at him, words failing her. His returning gaze was warmer than she deserved for her rudeness, and she offered a weak smile.

"I was at Ted's place when she walked over. She said she wasn't dressed for riding a tractor."

"She was wearing jeans!"

Kyle shrugged. "I didn't think that much about it, I just drove the tractor across the road." He flicked his eyes over her and she pulled the blanket tighter. He took his time meeting her gaze again, and when he did, his smile was warm and interested. Was that wishful thinking on his part, or hers?

He raised his hand as if he might touch her arm, then changed his mind and waved instead as he stepped back. "I'll go now. It was nice to see you again."

She bit her lower lip as he turned and walked down the steps toward the gravel drive. He stepped past her car, and she realized he was departing on foot.

"Kyle?"

He turned in surprise and angled his head to the side in a silent response.

"Where are you going?"

"I just live down at the corner, in the old school house. I'm fixing it up. You should come by." And with that he turned and ambled down the drive, soon obscured by heavy oak branches. Laney stood in the doorframe watching for a few minutes, blanket wrapped around her shoulders, oblivious to the winter cold.

———

SHE DIDN'T RETURN to the couch until after dinner. Claire and Evie arrived home at the same time, and the afternoon swept by in a flurry of outdoor fun, indoor decorating and holiday baking. Laney didn't have a chance to talk to her mother about the meddling earlier, and as she sank into the soft cushions, wrapped once again in the afghan, she no longer felt the urgency. A day with Connor and Max was more exhausting than a 24-hour shift at the hospital.

Evie walked into the family room from the kitchen carrying two steaming mugs. "Chamomile tea? You look zonked."

Laney nodded and waved her hand at the coffee table. "Put it there, I'm too tired to even hold the cup right now. Your kids are full-on."

Evie giggled. "I know, right? They keep me on my toes."

"Mom putting them to bed?"

"Yep. She's a godsend."

"For you, maybe."

"What? Oh no, what did she do?"

Laney groaned, pushed herself into a sitting position, and reached for her tea. "She got Kyle to drive the tractor across the road today."

She expected shock or dismay, but Evie just pursed her lips.

"Come on, that was inappropriate."

Evie shook her head. "No, I get it. You've got stuff there you need to work through, and it's not happening if you pretend he doesn't exist."

Laney gaped at her sister. *Traitor.* "There's nothing to work through. He's an ex-boyfriend. It's awkward because it didn't end amicably. I've learned my lesson."

"Avoidance isn't resolution."

"It's been twelve years, our relationship is most definitely resolved."

"So you've moved on, healed your heart, fallen in love again?"

"Love is overrated." Laney willed herself to stay calm. "I've moved on and found satisfying relationships, yes."

"Really?"

"Absolutely."

"Tell me about your boyfriends."

Laney wrinkled her nose.

"See? You don't even like the word."

They were interrupted just then by footsteps coming down the stairs, but Laney didn't feel any relief. Evie on her own was one thing, but her sister and mother together would put on the full-court press. She thought of Kyle's invitation. Should she stop in and visit? She didn't agree that there was anything left to talk about, but she could acknowledge that it probably wasn't healthy to be tense about a college boyfriend more than a decade later.

"Anyone want some cookies?" Claire hovered in the doorway.

Laney kept her eyes trained on her lap, watching her fingers worry the loose knit of the afghan. She didn't want to catch her mother's eyes just yet, didn't want to invite her into a conversation Laney herself would prefer to get out of before it went any further. She didn't want to be rude, though, and snack prep would buy a few more minutes. "Mmmm. Yes, please. Thanks, Mom."

Evie waved their mother off and scooted to the edge of her seat, leaning toward Laney.

"You can't tell me that you want to be alone forever."

That pulled her up short. The last time she had used that word, she had been lying in Kyle's bed. The decade in between faded away and she stood in the tiny one-bedroom apartment in Windsor, watching her younger self unwind naked limbs from Kyle's lean frame.

"This is perfect. I'd like to stay in this moment forever."

"You could stay forever. You could marry me."

"You know I need to go to Harvard. It's just for a year."

"You could stay and do your master's degree here."

"And what if that's not enough? What if I don't get into medical school again? This is Harvard, Kyle. A once in a lifetime opportunity. I have to go."

"What about us?"

"You could come with me."

"I just got hired at the school board, you know I can't leave."

"Then I'll be home on holidays, and you can come visit me at March Break. You'll be able to concentrate on teaching, and then we'll be reunited for good next summer."

"And then you'll marry me."

"And then I'll marry you."

She hadn't told Evie that they were going to get married. Kyle had never officially proposed or given her a ring, and two weeks after that conversation, he abruptly broke up with her, telling Laney that a year apart was too much to ask. She had been devastated, and when it came time to apply to medical schools the following year, she only chose universities out of the province.

"Hey, where'd you go?" Evie waved a hand in front of Laney's face.

She blinked hard and shook her head. "Sorry, I'm more tired than I thought."

Her sister raised an eyebrow, but sat back in her chair and didn't say anything else until their mother brought in a plate of chewy ginger molasses cookies. "Mom, I was thinking that I should take the boys into the city tomorrow to do a bit of last-minute shopping, do you want to come along?"

Claire looked at Laney and hesitated.

"Go with them, Mom. I'll catch up on some sleep. I have a bit of work to do too, I'll get that out of the way and then we'll have an entire week without any distractions."

Claire nodded and took a cookie. She might want to meddle, but for whatever reason she was giving that a pass tonight and Laney decided not to tempt fate. She gave her mom a tight squeeze, stole a cookie and plodded off to bed.

4

Kyle stepped into line behind Mrs. Wilkins and piled his groceries on the conveyor belt. He hadn't slept well. Next stop was Bun in the Oven for coffee.

"Hello, Kyle. School's out now?"

"Mrs. Wilkins. Yes, the kids are off until after New Year's." He edged forward in line and nodded at Karen, who gave him a wink. "Hey."

"Hey to you too." His friend gave him an amused look. "Did you hear that Laney's in town for the holidays?"

He rocked back on his heels. He didn't want to talk about Laney. He wouldn't mind talking to her, but he didn't want to contribute to idle chatter.

"Is that why you're buying fruits and vegetables?" Mrs. Wilkins ever so helpfully offered.

Kyle looked down at his purchases. Strawberries, croissants, lettuce, balsamic vinegar, a baguette, olives, whipping cream and a bag of two-bite brownies. He furrowed his brow. "I eat vegetables."

Karen pointed out that he usually bought apples and cucumbers, and she didn't remember him ever buying fancy vinegar. Kyle decided he might go straight home and make himself coffee there instead of risking further appraisal by the amateur detectives of Wardham.

"Just ring it up."

"Touchy, touchy," Karen said. "So I can't ask you about dropping off the tractor?"

"Jesus Chr—"

"Kyle Nixon!" Mrs. Wilson had moved toward the door with her groceries tucked into a basket on wheels, but she whirled around with surprising speed and wagged her index finger.

"Watch your language, young man, or I'll report you to the principal."

Kyle couldn't help but laugh. "Yes ma'am, my apologies."

Karen gave him a wry smile, but returned to scanning and bagging. *Saved by the wrath of a senior citizen.*

As he drove away from the store in his pickup truck, he considered his grocery choices. He honestly had just wandered the store, thinking with his stomach, but maybe a small part of him hoped that at some point over the next few days, he might get to cook Laney a meal. He wanted a chance to apologize to her. For years, he'd believed she'd left him and never looked back, and now he knew better.

After moving to the old school house the previous summer, Kyle had started running into Claire with regular frequency. At Ted's annual Labour Day picnic, he made the mistake of referring to her as the mother of the woman who broke his heart, and that opened the mama bear floodgates. Kyle had stood in Ted's yard while tiny Claire Calhoun, with her perfect silver blonde bob and disarmingly pleasant smile, poked her index finger into his solar plexus and told him that better be the only time he'd ever said that awful lie. When he turned red and scuffed his foot on the ground, she reached up, took firm hold of his chin and stared him in the eye with a fierceness he would never forget. "Kyle Nixon, you better make sure that everyone in this town thinks the best of my daughter. You hear me? I like you, but I won't hesitate to tell the parents at your school that you used to sneak into my house in the middle of the night."

It had taken everything in him to nod instead of smirk. Kyle doubted that anyone would care that he'd slept with his college girlfriend a million years ago, but there was a kernel of truth in what Claire said. He was only a year older, but he had been the more experienced between them. He was Laney's first. She'd wanted him to be her only, and he had promised her the moon to get in her pants.

He hadn't lied about loving her, wanting to marry her, being together forever, but in the end, that hadn't been enough. He'd thought it was just a break, but when she didn't come home the next summer, and then went east for medical school, he knew the split was permanent, and as time passed, he forgot that he was the one responsible. It took him a long time to move on. He dated casually for a few years, pretending to enjoy his bachelorhood. Actually, he had enjoyed sowing his wild oats, and he made some good friends, but every summer he was reminded of that too-short season when he finally had Laney before he lost her again. Every fall he'd slowly get back into the routine, only to spend Christmas hoping to run into her, wondering if she was at the farm. For five years his life was stuck in a holding pattern. When he heard she was moving from Halifax to Calgary, he crawled into a bottle of Jack Daniels, and almost went home with a blonde whose eyes weren't quite the same shade of ice blue, but close enough to pretend. When he called her Laney and got slapped for the mistake, something snapped into place. That wasn't who he was or what he wanted.

Another five years went by before he saw Laney at her father's funeral, and his world tipped upside down again.

———

LANEY STOOD on the porch outside the kitchen door, watching as her family headed off to do their last minute shopping. She could have gone with them after all, because she'd woken early and had already submitted her blog posts for the upcoming week and scheduled a few tweets about the children who would benefit from the New Year's Eve gala, but after the non-stop chatter about Lego and video games over breakfast, she decided to stick with her original plan. Remembering the bag of presents she'd left in her car the day before, she moved down the steps. The snow crunched under her feet, bright white under the clear winter sky. She pressed a button on her key fob and the car doors unlocked with a loud click. She paused for a moment, taking in the utter stillness of winter farm life. It pleased her. Chicago was always so busy. Noisy.

Maybe she needed to buy a cottage.

As she gazed across the front forty acres, a silver pickup truck pulled up to the old school house. She stopped and watched as Kyle hopped out. He was 300 yards away, but she knew it was him. He started toward his little house, but then stopped and turned. Was he looking at her? Could he see her if she didn't move? She raised her hand to give a tentative wave. It took a moment, but he waved back, then went inside.

She did the same. Her heart was racing and she knew her face was flushed. She shoved the presents under the Christmas tree and paced to the kitchen. She looked at the door. Her keys were hanging on a hook between the door and the window. A lump formed in her throat. What was she thinking? Good lord, what was she feeling? She wanted to see him again, up close this time. She shivered as raw desire rolled through her body. The open invitation to go over and be with him, just for a little while, was irresistible. She was nineteen again, making excuses to spend time with her sister's friends, desperate to feel the prickly sensation of his very nearness.

Don't do this. You're just going to get hurt. She stood there for a few minutes, having an internal battle royale. Going over to his house would open Pandora's box. *Didn't Evie flip that latch already?*

If she was honest, it wasn't Evie's fault. The conversation with

Rick had played over and over in her head on the drive from Chicago. Since when was she so cavalier with other people's feelings? She might not like emotions herself, but they were important to others. Maybe she did need to talk to Kyle, figure out why she felt so much about him and not enough about others. Find some balance, or at the very least, closure.

Mind made up, heart pounding, she grabbed her keys and headed out the door before she lost her courage.

———

KYLE PUT the groceries away and started a pot of coffee. It had taken all of his self-control not to jump back in the truck after that tentative wave. He had to wait until she was ready to talk. If she wanted to, she'd come to him. The crunch of tires on snow caused something deep in his gut to clench and he moved to the front door, narrowly beating Buddy. The border collie knew better than to bark, but he seemed to think it was his responsibility to screen all visitors. Kyle had come to love that about his furry roommate, but this particular guest he wanted all to himself. He snapped his fingers and pointed to the dog bed next to the wood stove.

Her footsteps stopped outside the entrance. He wouldn't let her chicken out. If she turned and walked away, he'd open the door, but he wanted her to be brave and knock. It took long enough that he knew she was nervous, but finally, two short taps announced her presence. He let out a deep breath, squared his shoulders, and opened the door with a welcoming smile.

"Hey..." Laney trailed off, glancing over her shoulder. "I saw you come home."

He nodded. "Want to come in?"

"Sure. Thanks." She stepped inside and took a tentative look around.

"Did you ever come in here before?"

"Once, as a teenager. It had been standing empty for a while at that point."

"It's a bit of a work in progress. I'm doing most of it myself, so it's slow going."

"It's nice, I like what you've done." She wrapped her arms around herself. Was she cold, or nervous? Probably both. The small talk felt weird.

Kyle stepped back to both gesture to the new kitchen space behind him, and to give her some room. "Do you want some coffee?" She nodded. "I just put on a pot."

Laney followed him into the open concept kitchen he had installed in one corner of the large open room. The refinished hardwood floors connected it to the rest of the space, but the dark espresso cabinets, granite countertops and stainless steel appliances stood out. He knew it was impressive, and he wasn't above strutting a bit for the girl who left Wardham to find success.

He turned to ask if she still took her coffee with lots of milk and sugar, but the words caught in his throat. Laney had shrugged off her coat and boots, and she was standing in his kitchen, looking at the photos stuck to the side of his refrigerator. She wore white socks, black yoga pants and an oversized white sweater which had slipped off one shoulder, revealing a thin elastic camisole strap. She looked perfectly at home, like they'd just had breakfast and were about to curl up on the couch and read together. Longing shot through Kyle's gut before he could brace himself against it. His roving gaze halted at the creamy expanse of skin between her shoulder and delicate jaw, his eyes devouring the shadow beneath her chin, the hollow at the base of her neck, the faint blue blood vessels tracing across the top of her chest. Her skin there was nearly translucent, and his fingers itched, remembering the bounce of her pulse, how warm and responsive she was under his touch.

No good would come of wanting her. But it couldn't be helped.

5

Laney didn't know who most of the people in the photographs were, but she stood there looking at them because she wasn't ready to look at Kyle yet. She hadn't expected his house to be such a home. For him to be so settled. So happy. When she wasn't, not really. She was satisfied with her life, and she loved her job, but there was still something missing. She hadn't made many friends yet in Chicago, something she would have to work on in the spring. She licked her lips and re-focused on the photos. She recognized Kyle's older brother Ian in a few of them, with a beautiful, curvy redhead and two small children. Other photos featured similar young families, probably friends Kyle had made after college. The top row of pictures featured his parents and younger sister. The middle photograph was larger than the others, and it looked like something out of a magazine.

"That's a nice picture of your whole family," Laney said quietly, keeping her eyes glued to the fridge. The other photos overlapped it slightly, but she could tell there was a brunette standing next to Kyle and faint jealousy pulsed in her chest.

The floor squeaked as he took a step toward her. "My mom hired a professional photographer to come out to their farm. That was two and a half years ago."

Another step. She turned enough to acknowledge his presence while still avoiding his gaze. He'd placed special emphasis on how old the photograph was. But yet here it was, on his fridge. She let her eyelids drift close for a moment. It was none of her business.

She felt the warmth of his fingers before they grazed the outside of her fist. The touch was brief and functional in nature, although her body didn't seem to get that message. She covered an unconscious sigh of pleasure with a polite smile and accepted the proffered mug of coffee from his other hand.

She sipped the sweet, hot liquid. She didn't put sugar in her coffee anymore, and the punch of nostalgia was more than she could bear. A single tear slipped down her cheek and she pinched her eyes closed, furious at herself.

He didn't say anything, turning instead to get himself a cup, when they were interrupted by a quiet whine from the living room. She jerked her head, and Kyle laughed as the whine was followed by a thump. "Buddy's been pretty patient, but I think he wants to meet you." He raised his voice slightly. "Okay, come here."

A medium sized black and white dog padded into view and Laney couldn't help but let out a happy sigh. "Hello there!" She dropped to her knees and let him sniff her all over. "Aren't you a quiet puppy. So patient. Yes, yes, you are. Good boy."

Above her, Kyle chuckled. She glanced up and her heart squeezed hard at the warm expression on his face. Buddy rubbed his nose into her shoulder, but he was just another reminder of how very different their lives had turned out. Laney didn't have a house plant, let alone a living, breathing dependent.

As if he sensed her growing unease, Kyle nodded to the other side of the kitchen island. "Want to sit? The wood stove is warmer over there."

He eased himself into the overstuffed armchair, leaving the matching couch for Laney. She appreciated the effort to give her some space. Buddy looked like he might hop up next to her, which she maybe wouldn't mind, but his human snapped his fingers and the collie ambled over to an oversized pillow nearby instead.

"It's been a long time, eh?" Kyle asked.

She nodded, still sipping her coffee.

"You're in Chicago now?"

Another nod. Another sip.

"How are you settling in? Do you…are you…"

She knew where the question was going, but after the picture on the fridge, she wasn't sure she wanted to share just how single she was. A quick glance around the open room didn't reveal any evidence of a woman. The only shoes on the rack at the door looked like Kyle's. One plate in the drying rack next to the sink. Familiar authors on the spines of his books that overflowed the shelves on either side of the large screen TV. Video game consoles neatly sat on the half-sized armoire beneath it. This was all him.

He tried again. "You didn't have anyone else to visit over the holidays?"

She arched one eyebrow.

"Sorry. None of my business."

"No, it's okay." His status didn't matter. *You're happy, remember? Show him that.* "Chicago is great. Everything you've probably heard and more. It's a dynamic city and I've lucked out with a really good practice. Some of my peers are still doing locums, and I've found a place to put down roots."

He offered an instant grin, wide and open, and she willed some of the tension out of her shoulders. "That sounds fantastic."

"How about you?" She waved her hand in a wide circle. "This is nice." He grinned wider again, waiting, and she couldn't help but return the smile. "Do you…are you…"

He shook his head. "Just me."

Laney pinched her lips together to restrain another smile from bursting forth. That news shouldn't warm her heart. At all. And it definitely shouldn't make her want to jump up and do a happy dance. *Or a lap dance.* She gave herself a mental slap. That was not at all where her mind should be going.

———

THE SINGLE TEAR in the kitchen had just about killed him. He was glad the conversation had continued, and now that they were talking, he wasn't in a hurry to get into anything heavy. "I'm glad you came over."

She took a deep breath. "Me too."

"Do you want to talk? Or just sit? I'm good with either."

"I don't know. Is it okay if we just sit for a while?"

"Of course."

He watched her relax into the couch, the wood stove providing the only soundtrack with an occasional pop and hiss.

"So." She swallowed hard. "Tell me about work. Where are you teaching now?"

The question surprised him. He was expecting to be asked more about the photo, dreading having to explain Crystal. Clearly she wanted to start on safer ground, and he should have known that she would. Laney never sought out drama.

"Wardham Elementary. I transferred seven years ago, and haven't looked back."

"You don't miss the city?"

Kyle shook his head. "I liked the learning experiences I gained teaching in a large urban school, but I missed the tight-knit community. And I wanted to be closer to my family."

"Tell me about your class."

"They're awesome. I've got a grade 5/6 split this year, and I really like that age. Inquisitive, able to do big projects, but not too hormone crazy just yet. I also teach science to the grade 4s, and they're fun too."

"Have you always taught the middle grades? You started with a grade 4 class, right?"

Kyle was touched that she remembered. "With one disastrous

exception, yes, I've always taught 4/5/6. The first year I taught here in Wardham, the only class that was available for me was grade 1. We all survived, but I was greatly relieved when Mrs. Schroeder retired the following year and I got her class."

"Oh my god, Mrs. Schroeder. She taught me grade 5."

"Me too," Kyle said, stretching his feet out toward the ottoman between them.

"I don't really remember you in elementary school."

"I remember you."

They both fell silent. Kyle knew she was thinking about her first year of high school. It was a story he both loved and hated. That's when she had first noticed him, hanging out with her sister and a bunch of other older students. Evie and Laney had always been close, and when a couple of other girls bristled at the nerdy grade nine student being invited to share lunch with the group, Kyle had smoothed it over with an easy smile, and asked her to sit next to him. He meant it as a protective gesture, but her crush was born that day, and persisted until her final year of university when she finally threw herself at him. He honestly had never realized how she felt, but at the first press of her body against his, he knew that ignorance must have been a self-defense mechanism because he was lost forever in a sea of Laney.

"You're right, it's been a long time." She stood up. "Is there more coffee?"

Kyle nodded and followed her into the kitchen. He couldn't help himself, he wanted to be close to her. He leaned his hip against the counter, watching her pour herself a cup. She added milk, but skipped the sugar. He raised an eyebrow, and she smiled.

"People change," she said.

"In some ways. You haven't changed that much in other ways." She was still beautiful. Maybe even more than ever. And every passing minute seemed to ping another memory of how they'd been together. Their natural chemistry and shared interests —naked and otherwise.

She shifted from one foot to the other. "Neither have you."

They stood there, staring at each other, and Kyle wanted to take the mug out of her hands and ease her against the counter. Press into her and show her that most of all, his attraction to her had never changed, that her mouth still drove him to distraction, her mind still made him crazy and her body still brought him to his knees.

A hiss of air dragged him out of his fantasy. He cleared his throat and shifted back, painfully aware that his state of arousal was on full display, and Laney had noticed. She dragged her gaze back up to his face, her eyes wide with a mix of desire and fear. He needed to back off, as much as he wanted to do the complete opposite. "Let's sit down again. I...there's something that I need to say to you, that's long overdue."

LANEY FOLLOWED Kyle to the sitting area, confused by the moment they had just shared in the kitchen. If he hadn't moved away from her, she probably would have launched herself onto his body and rubbed up against him like a cat in heat. She hadn't felt this overwhelmed by lust since they were together in college. She thought she had outgrown such feelings, but apparently not. She pressed her thighs together as she curled up on the couch again. She ached from hip to hip, inflamed with desire and dying for Kyle to touch her.

"I owe you an apology."

She didn't know what she was expecting Kyle to say, but that wasn't it. An odd tightness pulled across her chest, her shoulders curling up and in like she was a hedgehog under attack. She breathed out, a quiet rush of air over her bottom lip reminding her she was staring, mouth open. She blinked, searching for something, anything to say. Nothing came to mind.

"Laney...dammit, stop looking at me like that. I don't want to hurt you, I want to free you. Free myself, if I'm being honest. Please just listen to me."

She nodded, not sure she'd heard everything over the pounding in her ears, but as much as it hurt, she also wanted to have that final conversation they'd never had.

"…and I think that's why it took me so long to get over you, because I was wallowing in pain. I thought you'd broken up with me. I was convinced you'd come back someday, and when you moved to Calgary, I knew it was finally over."

She was on her feet, shaking from head to toe, before she realized rage had taken over. "Excuse me? What the kind of apology is this, Kyle?" Laney swiped at hot tears now freely sliding down her cheeks.

She stalked toward him, counting on her fingers the points he had missed. "First, you broke up with me. You broke *my* heart, asshole. I asked you to wait for me and you said it was too much. Second, I tried to talk to you, you wouldn't come to the phone or answer my emails. Third—"

"I never read them," Kyle muttered, so low she almost missed it.

"Then that's the third point." She stopped in front of him, bitter, angry defenses all in place, ready to do battle. "Fourth, if you think that I'm going to absolve you, free you, whatever that means, you've got another thought coming, mister, because I will never forgive you for ruining love for me."

6

Somehow, he'd bungled this up. That barely scratched the surface of how colossally wrong he'd gone about this conversation, actually. Kyle wanted to press pause and re-group, but Laney was unleashed and there was no going back. It was killing him to hear how much pain she'd held inside for so long, but she needed to let it out, needed to make him hear what he'd avoided as a younger man.

Realizing that she was spent, at least momentarily, Kyle reached for her hands and tugged her down so she was sitting on the ottoman in front of him. "I ruined love for me too, you know. And I'm so sorry I did that. I shouldn't have said all of that before, it doesn't matter. I was just trying to explain why it took me so long to realize that our breakup was my fault. But I know that it was, and I'm sorry that I did that to you. You didn't deserve it."

She stared at their hands, fingers still twisted together. He wanted to do something more, hug her or wipe away her tears, but he worried that she might bolt if pushed too far. His Laney of long ago had been free with her emotions, full of love and passion, easy to rile up, fun to spar with, but also happy to be soothed by lovemaking. It was his fault that this flood of anger was now so foreign to her that she didn't know how to cope. He'd stolen more than her love.

Kyle pushed against that regret, shaking his head. He could wallow once she had gone; right now he had some making right to do. "Laney—" his voice was strained, and he cleared his throat. "Sweetheart, you can let it all out. Hit me. Flog me up and down Main Street. I can take it."

"I've never admitted that before," she said, her voice quiet. "To myself, I mean. I thought I didn't *want* to love anyone—I thought it was my choice."

Kyle took a chance and pulled her into his lap. Twelve years hadn't changed a thing, their bodies still fit together perfectly, even though she was coiled tighter than a rattlesnake. He stroked up and down her spine through the soft sweater, willing her to relax, until she eased her head onto his shoulder. Inch by inch, her entire body settled into his, and he felt the top layer of her tension ebb away. Leaning back, he closed his eyes and hoped that the warmth between their bodies felt as healing for Laney as it did for him. She curled her arm across his chest, and with a sigh, relaxed fully. For the first time since she'd arrived, Kyle felt completely comfortable. Exhausted and sad, but comfortable. He'd take it.

———

THEY SAT like that for almost an hour. At one point, Kyle was convinced that she had fallen asleep, but he didn't want to risk losing the moment, and he couldn't see her face without shifting. Her head was tucked under his chin, and he didn't mind, because her hair smelled amazing, an intoxicating blend of honey and some kind of fruit. Thank god her ass was perched high on his thigh and her legs were bent over his other arm, because in the space beneath he had developed a brutal erection. He couldn't remember ever being this turned on by cuddling before, except maybe in those first few weeks of dating when they were still working on rounding all the bases.

He remembered every single day of that spring, the long string of her firsts: Laney slowly peeling off her t-shirt in the barn, then crossing her arms against her chest; her sliding across the bench in his truck, straddling him, grinding her jean-clad pussy against his cock; getting completely naked in a hotel room after the Science Society Formal Ball, wanting to punch a hole in the wall after their only condom broke. Laney had made that night worthwhile anyway, sliding his cock between their bodies, holding herself open, rubbing against the length of him until they both shattered apart. They'd spent the night twisted up in each other, and when Laney wrapped her warm little hand around him in the shower the next morning, he thought he'd died and gone to heaven. He returned the pleasure before check out, and two weeks later when he moved into his first apartment, they had an entire box of condoms at the ready.

She lifted her head and he was torn between wanting her to see where he had wandered in his mind, and hoping she'd return to her original position so he could keep smelling her hair like a pervert. He didn't dare think that she might be wandering around the same spots on memory lane, even when she pressed her forehead against his chin, then rubbed up his face until her lips connected with his jaw. Kyle stifled a groan and eased her legs down to the ground, freeing his arm to press between their bodies.

"Laney, sweetheart, that's not a good idea." *It's brilliant, asshole, shut up.* He could barely grind out the words. His body was not on board with being noble.

"Probably not." She pressed against his hand, flat against her upper chest, stretching her body to reconnect with his face, and the upper swell of her breast filled his palm. This time the groan was louder. "Tell me to stop."

"We're going to regret this." Freud would have a field day with what was going in his head. Baser instincts were definitely gaining traction.

"Probably. Tell me to stop." Her lips found the corner of his mouth, at an angle, and then her face turned again and they were sharing the barest of open mouth kisses, her bottom lip resting on his, pressing it down. Her eyes were wide, pupils dark and full of want. He didn't see any hesitation, only heat, and his resolve slipped. *One kiss.* He let her breath slip into his mouth, hot and moist, and he was lost, disoriented in a mixed fog of memories and unfulfilled fantasies.

With a slight jerk, his extended arm relaxed, allowing Laney to crawl back on his lap, straddling his hips this time, and she looked down at his erection with a smirk. "I knew you didn't want me to stop."

"Wanting you to stop and knowing you should are two different things. Hell no, I don't want you to stop." He dragged a ragged breath into his chest and ran his hands down the sides of her body, squeezing her hips, tracing over her thighs and then up again, harder this time, sliding his palms under her sweater and over the thin cotton tank top hiding underneath. "But I don't want you to hate me, either."

"I'm not an innocent college kid anymore, Kyle." She wiggled her hips, trying to slide closer to the bulge in his jeans. "I like sex. You make me think of sex. I'm all fired up from fighting. Let's go."

It should have been an ardour-dousing wakeup call, the casual offer of something that was once so special to her, to them. The higher-thinking part of his brain was protesting that something was wrong, that Laney couldn't possibly want a booty call.

But all Kyle could focus on was the easy confidence that she had gained, how she must have gained it, and his primal need to re-possess that which he had lost took over. He could hear raspy need in his voice and he didn't care. "Now it's your turn to tell me to stop, sweetheart."

———

LANEY GASPED as Kyle wrenched her sweater up her torso and buried his face against her camisole. His breath was hot through the fabric, and while she couldn't see what he was doing because her sweater was bunched between her chin and his head, she could feel his mouth moving up and around her body in a slow arc. By the time he was at her ribs, his hands had wrapped around to her ass, and she rocked against his cock. Helpless against her desire, she heard herself whimper at the contact and rolled her hips again, this time deliberately, seeking out the delicious tweak of something on his jeans against her clit. The edge of his fly, maybe. Back and forth she flicked her body, flexing her thighs to give her more leverage, constrained by his fierce hold on her hips and his head pressed firmly now into the side of her breast, his mouth approaching her right nipple.

She pulled her sweater over her head, tossing it to the floor. Breathing hard, she watched as Kyle yanked her camisole down as far as he could between her breasts. Through hooded eyes, dark and pulsing, he took in the slight swells.

"You're my every fantasy, Laney. So fucking beautiful."

Did he mean it? She felt more wanted in that moment than she had in a long time. She hadn't allowed herself to think about Kyle, had convinced herself early on that the passion she remembered in his bed was magnified through the distorting lens of puppy love. That had probably been the right decision for her self-preservation, but since stepping into his house, there was no doubt she'd been absolutely wrong. Every orgasm she'd had over the last twelve years paled in comparison to getting to second base with Kyle.

She ran her index finger under his chin, pulling his gaze to meet hers. Her thumb brushed his lower lip, then pushed in, letting his teeth nip at her. She stared at him, wanting to soak up the details. He held her gaze, his eyes hot and lusty as his tongue slowly laved the pad of her thumb. The slow, deliberate swipes synchronized with his palms on her nipples, and a tremor wracked her body. She took a deep breath, then shrugged, and he followed her wordless instruction, pulling her camisole down to her waist. He cupped her breasts, obviously admiring the pale pink swells plumped in his hands.

Nobody had ever made her feel this beautiful, this wanted. Her nipples begging for his attention. He drew one peak into his mouth, sucking and nibbling, until she surged her entire body toward his head with a moan.

"That's my greedy girl." His words were loaded with possessive pride, and she nodded despite herself, cheeks pink with excitement.

Kyle wrapped one arm under her ass and pushed to his feet in one fluid motion. Laney gasped and wrapped her legs tight around his waist. Her pussy clenched at the loss of contact. She was so wet he could probably feel it through her yoga pants. She buried her face in his neck, and he murmured in her ear that he was going to put her down on the bed for a minute. As she sank into a soft grey bedspread, she realized he had carried her into a makeshift bedroom on the far side of the entrance. He stepped out, disappearing behind the curtain that blocked off his sleeping area, and she was alone. Half-naked, on her ex-boyfriend's bed. He was still fully clothed and now gone, and her nerve slipped, spurring her to wrap her arms across her chest.

Kyle stepped back into view, holding a condom. Something about her pose caused him to pause, and he slowly crawled onto the bed, dropping the condom before stopping above her. "Where'd my greedy girl go? Don't cover up, Laney. We've been through this, remember? It just gives me another layer to peel away."

She did remember, then, the first time that Kyle had come to visit her at the farm when her family wasn't home. She'd invited him up to her bedroom and he'd said it would probably be a better idea to go for a walk. They'd gotten as far as the barn, and she'd pulled off her t-shirt. She didn't need a bra then. Could still get away without one, although she'd come to appreciate them more with age. That afternoon, desire had only taken her so far, but after Kyle had wiggled her out from behind her arms, he'd used his mouth and hands to convince her that naked breasts were a good thing for both of them.

No convincing required this time. She took a big breath and slid her arms over her head, grasping for a non-existent headboard. Stretching under his gaze was foreplay in itself. He was looking at her like she was a crazy expensive steak dinner. Kyle lowered his head to her nipples, alternating licks and whispering puffs of hot air on them until she was twisting beneath him, begging for him to help her.

"Help you? You're going to need to be more specific than that, sweetheart."

"I want you," Laney panted. "Inside me. I want you inside me."

Kyle reached for her hands pawing at his shoulders and returned them above her head, anchoring them this time to the pillow. "Don't let go."

He swept down her body, grabbing the waist of her yoga pants and tugging them down over her hips and off her legs as he staggered off the bed. He jerked his t-shirt over his head, and Laney got what felt like her first sight of his naked torso. His body was familiar to her, but time had hardened the planes of his chest, and he now had more hair there, and trailing lower. Kyle sucked in a breath as her gaze stopped at the button on his jeans, and she almost surged off the bed as he flicked it open.

"Stay there. Just watch."

She slumped back against the pillow, panting, legs twitching, devouring the sight of Kyle slowly undoing his zipper, then his faded blue jeans dropping to the floor, and he moved toward her again, wearing just a pair of black boxer briefs that did nothing to disguise how much he wanted her.

———

SHE SPRAWLED in front of him on the bed in a pair of skimpy black boy shorts, her legs spread wide, her pink nipples pointing straight at the ceiling, but all Kyle could see at that particular moment were her ice blue eyes, full of need. He was a bastard for taking advantage of that, but unless she changed her mind, he wasn't going to stop. He only had one option and had to hope that it was enough.

"I'm going to make this good for you, sweetheart."

Her whispered response just about brought him to his knees. "I know."

He nuzzled the hollow below her ribcage, tracing ever so carefully around her sensitive belly button, his palm on one side, his face on the other. She shivered, and he circled her navel again.

"You remember."

"Oh, yeah." He knew that she was ticklish on her hips, and couldn't resist wiggling his fingers a bit as he peeled back her underwear. He shot her a wolfish smile of appreciation at the sight of her blond curls before sliding his hands, tangled in her panties, down her legs. As she kicked the last of her clothing off her toes, he stroked up her legs, pausing for a moment to squeeze the tender flesh behind her knees. A whimper confirmed that still made her clit twitch, and his grin widened. Yeah, he remembered.

He pushed himself between her legs, rasping his rough cheek against her upper thigh.

"Don't close your eyes, sweetheart. This is the good part."

"It's all pretty good."

He chuckled, and lowered his face to nuzzle her pussy lips, stroking inside with his tongue, then flicking her clit. She was soaking wet already, and she convulsed around the first finger he slipped into her. He added a second, moving inside her, matching that pace as he sucked and flicked her nub. It didn't take long for her breathing to speed up, and as she approached her first orgasm she started moaning with each exhale. Kyle urged her on, telling her how gorgeous she was, how much he liked her taste, until she cursed him to stop talking and get back to sucking. He hummed his agreement against her clit until she stumbled over that cliff, wrapping her legs around his head, all of her twitching in release.

As she oozed back onto the bed, he shed his boxers and reached for the condom, but Laney shook her head.

"Let me taste you first."

Oh, hell yes. He couldn't take much of her hot little mouth without exploding, but he needed to feel her tongue on him for just a minute before he covered up.

"Can I let go of the pillow now?" Laney twisted her lips into an innocent smile, but the fire in her eyes told the truth. She wanted to be in charge for this part, but she was going to let him give her that instead of taking it.

He nodded and she slithered up and around him, wrapping him in her intoxicating scent. That damn shampoo again, but also her arousal, mingling in a heady combination. She kissed him, tasting herself, and he groaned into her mouth. She pulled him to the edge of the bed and knelt on the floor between his legs. She'd only done this a few times over their summer together, and always with nervous hesitation. New Laney was confident in her appraisal of his cock.

"Like what you see?"

"Mmm hmm." She leaned forward and rubbed her face along his shaft, then ever so slowly drew him into her open mouth, swirling her tongue around his wide head. Her small hands caressed up his thighs to join her mouth, one curving around his base to match the motion of her tongue, the other reaching lower to squeeze his balls.

It was possibly the best thing he'd ever felt in his entire life, but he knew the main course would be even better, so he reluctantly tugged her to her feet. She stumbled against him, her hand still wrapped about his erection, and after he ripped the condom from its foil package, she helped sheath him.

"I think this is where I say stop and you explode," Laney teased.

Kyle growled and yanked her into the cradle of his hips. "I would stop. I'd probably jerk off, but I'd stop touching you. Is that what you want me to do, sweetheart? Keep my hands to myself?"

"Don't you dare." She shoved him farther back on the bed and straddled him, notching his cock against her ready slit. As his eyes grabbed hers, she sank on to him, wrapping him in her incredible wet warmth. He cupped her ass, shifting her pelvis to accept him to the root, and her legs twisted tight around his body. Their fingers melded together, providing leverage as they rocked back and forth, slowly at first, then faster at Laney's urging. Kyle didn't want to hurry to the finish, fearing that she would shutter herself as soon as they unwound their bodies, but as his erection swelled inside her, he knew he'd be joining her as she started to come around him.

"You fill me up," Laney whispered against his lips as he surged into her one last time, and then he did, and she giggled.

7

L aney knew that Kyle needed to deal with the condom, but she didn't want to climb off his lap just yet. As he reached between them, she lifted her hips to give him clearance, then settled back to rest on his hard thighs. This clinging was out of character, and she should feel unsettled, but she'd just had the best sex of her life, with an ex-boyfriend she'd spent the last decade pretending didn't exist, in his adorable half-finished, renovating-by-himself one room school house. Unsettled wouldn't even begin to describe how Laney *should* be feeling, and it didn't matter, because how she *actually* felt was pretty damn good.

Kyle leaned back, his gaze wandering over her face. "Are you hungry?"

She nodded and slid to the side. She wrapped herself in the bedspread as Kyle headed for the kitchen. It had been a long time since she'd had middle of the day sex. Even longer since she'd wanted to linger afterward and share food and conversation.

"What do you want to drink?" Kyle called from around the corner.

"Water is fine!"

"Still or sparkling?"

The question shouldn't send her into a laughing fit, but the last time Kyle had made a post-coital snack it had featured cold pizza and flat ginger ale. Times had changed indeed. She tipped onto her side. The scratching of nails on the hardwood floor warned her that Buddy was on his way to investigate the problem, and when he slid to a stop at the foot of the bed it sent her into another round of laughter. When Kyle returned, carrying a tray of fruit and croissants, she was still pressing a hand to her quivering abdomen.

"I take it that you didn't expect me to have sparkling water?" Kyle cocked an eyebrow at her as he settled next to her.

"Ahhhh, God...I don't know why that was so funny. It's not. It's just..." Laney gestured at the bed. "This was so familiar, you know? You are..." She wasn't finding a better word for it, so she just re-used the same one. "*You* are so familiar. It's surreal when I think about all that has happened since the last time we slept together, and yet that part felt so..."

Kyle nodded, as if in agreement that it was in fact so *something*. He cleared his throat and grinned. "It wasn't all familiar. You've gotten a lot more comfortable with some things."

"Oh, that." She blushed.

"Don't be embarrassed." His eyes crinkled as he bit into a croissant. "It was awesome."

"I'm not embarrassed, exactly. I'm surprised at myself." She could count the number of times she'd offered oral sex on one hand. Until today, she had never understood the appeal. "But it felt right in the moment."

"Felt more than right. Your mouth is wicked, Laney Calhoun." He reached out and dragged his thumb across her bottom lip, sending a wave of heat crashing through her belly.

"My roommate during med school worked in a woman-friendly sex shop, I attended a few of her classes." Her blush deepened. "I don't know why I shared that."

"It's okay. I know you've had other relationships, so have I. It's not a big deal."

Laney's hand froze over the strawberries. Her chest felt tight, like the weight of all of Kyle's girlfriends had just been dropped on her. "Yeah, right."

"Laney?"

"What?"

He gave her a curious look, she could feel it hot against her cheek even though she refused to meet his gaze. "Is it a big deal?"

She focused all of her attention on the berries. There was a big one in the middle that looked yummy, but it would probably be too much to eat in one bite. She moved it out of the way, looking for its smaller cousin.

"Laney." Kyle moved closer and placed his hand flat against her bare back.

She nodded. "It's nothing."

"Clearly."

"So you've had…relationships? Since me? I mean, of course you have, but they've been serious?" She shifted a bit to see Kyle's face. He was hard to read, but he didn't look upset, just confused.

"Yeah. I dated a bit after we broke up, and then a few years ago I was in a serious relationship. You haven't dated?"

She shrugged. "I've dated, I guess. Evie pointed out that I don't like the word boyfriend, and she's right. I haven't been interested in anything emotional in a long time. Too messy."

"Haven't been interested, or scared of the risk?" Kyle's appraising look reminded her that they'd shared some brutal honesty earlier.

She sighed. "You sound like Evie. Not wanting to get hurt again doesn't need to be about fear."

"I didn't mean it like that. I was actually accused of the opposite. That I think I want a committed relationship when I really don't, that I'm scared to be alone."

"Is that true?"

"I don't think so. But I haven't dated in two years now, kind of an experiment of sorts."

Laney couldn't keep the shock off her face. "Two years?"

It was Kyle's turn to shrug. "I had some stuff to work out. Why, how long has it been for you?"

She busied herself with choosing another strawberry. No way was she answering that.

Kyle chuckled. "So, less than that, eh?"

Time to change the subject. "The serious girlfriend … she's the one in the photo on the fridge?"

Kyle nodded. "Crystal. We dated for a couple of years."

"What happened?"

"I don't know if we should talk about it."

"Why not?"

"Because I'm hoping we might have sex again, and I'm pretty sure that if we keep talking about my ex, that won't happen."

Laney laughed, and let it go. His plan was better. So much better. She moved the tray off the bed and slithered up Kyle's body until all the necessary bits fit together.

8

____

Two hours later, Laney stepped out of the shower at the farmhouse. Kyle had suggested they shower together at his place, but she knew she needed to get home before her family returned or Evie would figure out how she had spent the morning. *And a decent chunk of the afternoon as well.* She grinned. Definitely not what her mother intended when she sent him across the road, but she finally felt like their breakup made sense. What they'd had was too big for either of them to handle, the combination of puppy love and intense chemistry overwhelming for young adults trying to find their individual paths. She once believed that love and chemistry were one and the same, and she blocked both out of her life, but today blew that idea out of the water. Laney wiped the condensation off the mirror and stared at herself. Her eyes were clear, her heart was calm. She didn't love Kyle. *But boy oh boy, has he raised the bar on awesome sex.* She peered at her reflection like it might be lying to her, but she knew it wasn't. She was content about her history for the first time in a long time. Slightly miffed that she'd let sex get so mechanical and routine, but otherwise at peace with the path from past to present. If Kyle hadn't broken up with her, she wouldn't have travelled across the country, might have stuck with her original plan of a family medicine practice in Wardham, wouldn't have discovered the magic of reconstructive surgery. He freed her, even if it was in a shitty and emotionally stunted way. And it seemed like he suffered for that just as much as she did. They'd both wasted enough time on regret.

From downstairs, her mother's voice carried up the stairs. "Laney? We're home."

"I'm just getting out of the shower! Be right down." She reached for a towel, wondering how soon she could pop over to the school house again.

The rest of that day and the next were dominated by Connor and Max. Part of Laney was disappointed that she didn't have any time to see Kyle again, but she convinced herself it was a small part, driven primarily by the delicious ache between her legs, and resolved to not care. Her nephews filled her time and attention with dragon-slaying and fort-building, and before she knew it, she was reading them a bedtime story for the second night in a row.

Downstairs, she found her sister taking a large castle out of its box.

"What are you doing?"

"Toy manufacturers hate parents. Did you know that? They think we don't suffer enough, so they package toys with unnecessary twist-ties, zip-ties and the occasional screw, all in the name of ruining Christmas morning."

"Uh…okay, I'm sorry I asked."

Evie blew a lock of hair out of her eyes and laughed. "Max is going to be desperate to play with this when he opens it, so I'm trying to eliminate the painful bouncing-yelling-whining that would happen if I need to release this thing from the clutches of packaging while he waits. Last year I had the same idea, but I did it on Christmas Eve. This year, I want everything done so tomorrow night can just be about carols and cocoa and an early bedtime."

"Living large in Wardham, eh?"

"Shut up, you like an early bedtime even more than me."

Laney curled up on the couch. "That's true. So...remember what we were talking about the other day?"

"Mom's meddling or how crazy my kids are? I'm familiar with both concepts."

"The first one. And that maybe I needed to talk to Kyle."

"Mm-hmm." Evie's head disappeared behind the back of the castle.

"Well, I did. I went over there yesterday and we talked. It was good." *And then we didn't, and that was even better.*

"Oh Laney..." Evie shoved the castle aside and pinned her under a heavy gaze. "It was good? Really? You're fine?"

"Really. I know, I asked myself the same thing. But yeah, I feel totally fine now. A bit silly for wasting so much time on bitterness, but knowing that he wasn't left unscathed...I don't know, we just..." *licked each other's wounds all better* "...came to an understanding."

"Well, that's good. I'm glad you've finally put him behind you."

Laney blushed, thinking that Kyle was the one who had put himself behind her the second time.

"You have, right? You need to move forward, not backward. The last thing I'd want is for Kyle to break your heart again."

She considered telling Evie what had really happened, but doubted that her sister would think it was quite as hot as she did. "Guaranteed, Ev, my heart is untouchable. If I hadn't learned that from Kyle, I did from you and Mom."

Claire wandered in just in time to catch the tail end of Laney's pronouncement. "Oh no, Laney, don't say that!"

"Why not? It's true. Love has done quite the number on both of you."

Evie tucked the castle into the box and grabbed a roll of wrapping paper. "Normally I'd agree with Mom, but in this case, whatever keeps you from falling in love with Kyle again is fine by me."

Claire's eyes twinkled and Laney groaned. "Thanks for that."

"Delaney, did you run into Kyle?"

She was so tempted to share all of the sticky, lurid details with her mom as payback for her initial meddling, except in the end it hadn't been such a bad plan at all. "You know I did. Since when are you afraid to drive a tractor?"

"I was wearing my new jeans and it looked greasy."

"Yeah, right. Well, that was awkward, when he showed up at the door, but then yesterday I went over to his place and we talked. It was less awkward and more..." *intimate* "...productive."

"I'm so glad, sweetheart. You've held onto that sadness for too long. But your sister is right to be worried. Kyle has always had a strong hold on your emotions. I want you to be free of that, not just trade love for hate and vice versa."

It was Laney's turn to blow hair out of her face this time. She was starting to get pissed off, a common theme in Calhoun late night chats. "Three things. First, I'm a grown-up, let me worry about my feelings, be they over the top or utterly lacking. Second, I. Am. Not. In. Love. With. Anyone. Love is still overrated and unnecessary. Third, I think it's time for cookies and tea, yes?"

She headed into the kitchen, but her sister and mother just followed. Escape was not going to be that easy.

"Laney, we just want you to be happy," Claire said.

"I *am* happy. I have a great job, and an interesting social life, and despite them being incredibly annoying, I even like my family. I finally settled my feelings about a long-ago ex-boyfriend and it's *still* not good enough for you both."

Evie reached past Laney to grab a teapot off the shelf. "You know, I wouldn't change a thing about my relationship with Dale."

Laney snorted.

"Really. He gave me two awesome kids. If I hadn't married him, I wouldn't have them."

"And I wouldn't have given up knowing and loving your dad, even though his death was so hard on me."

Laney looked at the beautiful, crazy women in front of her. "Of course, you say that now. But from my perspective, if having kids means dealing with a deadbeat ex-husband, or if having a grand love affair means someone suffers through a year of depression at the end of it … it's probably safer to stick to being a party of one."

Claire pulled her daughter in for a gentle hug. "I wish I could explain just how wrong you are, sweetie, but it might be something that you need to experience for yourself."

"Isn't that what losing Kyle was? And now I've moved on. As you wanted me to, remember."

"You were young. I want you to have a meaningful adult relationship."

Laney's jaw twitched. "Not that young. Too young to make it work, maybe, but not too young to know what it was."

Claire paused, knowing she'd pushed her daughter to her limit. "Okay. I'm sorry. You're right, this is none of my business."

Evie busied herself with putting spelt cookies on a plate, and the tension ebbed.

9

Christmas Eve morning at the Calhoun farm started with group Pilates. Laney thought about bowing out and going for a run by herself instead, but Connor promised that "Ninja Monster Pilates is way different than boring Mom Pilates, don't worry!" And he was right. Max sat on her abs while she did The Hundred, and Connor challenged her to beat him in double leg lifts. She couldn't. Humbled by an eight year old.

After inhaling plain yogurt and homemade granola for breakfast, everyone pitched in to prep food for the next two days. Calhouns never procrastinated, and holiday meals were no exception. Claire set to work on stuffing and pie for Christmas dinner, while Evie and the boys prepped clam chowder for that night. That left the traditional Christmas Eve bread pudding for Laney, but when she went to get a loaf of bread from the pantry, Evie and Claire exchanged guilty looks.

"You didn't get extra bread?"

"We decided to have fruit salad for dessert instead," Evie said. "Bread pudding is so excessive."

"You're a lunatic. It's Christmas, we're having bread pudding. I'll run into town, do we need anything else? What else were you thinking of eliminating from the menu?"

———

IT HAD BEEN years since Laney had last driven into Wardham, but it looked pretty much the same. She parked in front of Wardham Grocery and paused on the sidewalk to take in her home town. A fancy bakery and coffee shop had opened up a few doors down, and the bank had been recently renovated, but otherwise it looked like the same place she spent her first 21 years.

Inside the grocery store, she recognized Karen Miller at the checkout. Karen's younger brother had been in Laney's grade in high school, and a few years after graduation had been drafted into the NHL. She wasn't sure if Karen would remember her or not, but offered a little wave to be friendly. It was returned, along with a surprised smile. She didn't know what to make of that, so she grabbed a cart and went in search of day-old bread.

Potato chips for the top of the cabbage casserole and marsh-mallows for the sweet potatoes, along with nibblies and ginger ale for the afternoon, completed her purchases. Laney was as health conscious as the next person, she was a doctor for goodness sake, but her sister went too far.

A display of pet accessories caught her eye. Maybe she should get Kyle and Buddy Christmas presents. It would just be neigh-bourly. She grabbed a purple Kong before she could change her mind and turned back to the previous aisle for peanut butter.

Kyle was harder to find something for in the grocery store, but as she moved down the soft drink aisle, she saw a display of energy drinks. Red Bull reminded her of the year before they started dating. Late night studying infused with sexual frustration and stolen glances. Playing Resident Evil just to have an excuse to sit next to him, her thigh rubbing against his, their forearms brushing as they worked through the levels together. A shiver raced up her spine, and she grabbed a four pack. It wasn't the worst Christmas present in the world, and it would be an excuse to stop at the school house.

It is an absolutely awful gift, but if we get naked, he probably won't care. The promise of quick and dirty sex spurred Laney toward the checkout counter. She grabbed a tin of mints and added it to her pile.

"Nice to see you again, Laney. Back for Christmas?"

"Hi, Karen. Yep, we're all at the farm."

"Have you seen Kyle?"

She did a double take. How was that anyone else's business, and why did Karen Miller care? "What? Why?"

"Everyone liked you two together."

"That was a long time ago. How much do I owe you?"

Karen took her time finding the total button. Laney wanted to throw a fifty at her and run. "I shouldn't have said anything, it's just…never mind."

Laney was still annoyed, but there wasn't anyone else in the store, and curiosity got the better of her. "Just what?"

"He hasn't dated in a while, and when your mom said that you were coming home for the holidays, we thought maybe it might be an opportunity for him to deal with your breakup."

"We who? You and my mom?" Laney couldn't believe her ears. The meddling in Wardham was reaching new heights, and her mother had a lot of explaining to do.

"Oh no! Right, you've been gone a while. Kyle's brother married Carrie, my best friend? Evie knows her. Anyway, it was one conversation, that's all." Karen was back-peddling hard. "I've really overstepped here, I'm sorry." She bit her lip, and Laney felt some of her anger slip away.

"Right. Well, I think everyone should probably just mind their own business. Kyle's a grown man, he can take care of himself."

It took another fifteen minutes for Laney to stash her groceries in the car and grab a latte from the bakery, because she was stopped by three people who wanted to tell her how happy they were she was visiting for the holidays and to ask if she'd seen Kyle yet. She considered stopping at the drugstore for a gift bag, but decided if she was going to have any time for a quickie, the presents should probably just be wrapped in a grocery bag.

She parked her car on the far side of the school house from her mom's farm. Not hiding where she was, but at the same time, she was quite done with questions for the day.

Kyle opened the door at the second knock. He raised his eyebrows and flashed a wide, easy smile. "Hey, you. I wasn't sure if…I thought you might be busy with family stuff."

"I have been." She held out the grocery bag. "I was shopping and decided to get you and Buddy some Christmas presents."

He pulled her inside and closed the door. He slid the package out of her grasp, placed it on a small table next to the entrance and closed the gap between them. "Thank you. I'll open it in a minute. But first—" He slid one hand behind her neck "—I'm going to kiss you, okay?"

He didn't wait for a response, but he didn't rush either. His other hand curled against her jaw, and she saw his lips part, his eyelids drop, his nose tilt away, and as his breath touched her mouth, everything slipped out of focus and it was all warm and muzzy and delicious.

Lips on lips. Lips parting, then tongues dancing, teeth nipping, then after breaking apart for ragged breaths, they crashed together again, hungry and needy.

"Open your present," she whispered, pressing her hips up and into his erection.

"Can I open you first?"

"It's related, trust me."

Kyle eased back enough to twist and grab the bag. "It's heavy for a sex toy."

She giggled. She didn't giggle, ever. Except, apparently, when around Kyle. Or maybe it was Wardham, although she didn't remember being this…whatever *this* was on previous trips. It was fun being this different Laney. He reached into the bag and pulled out the four-pack. "Red Bull?"

"You used to love the stuff."

"When we had to pull all-nighters, studying. I haven't drunk it in years."

"It reminded me of you." Laney angled toward him, stealing a quick kiss. She ignored the worry that whispered in the back of her mind. Why was this so easy? Fuck it, she didn't care. "Keep going."

"Okay. Thank you, for the Red Bull. Maybe I'll go on a road trip in the summer."

Come to Chicago. Her heart thumped. That was lunacy. This was a bit of fun to get Kyle out of her system. She didn't want to start anything up again. She'd sworn as much to her sister and mother, and she'd been telling the truth. Her stomach twisted, and she swallowed hard.

He pulled out the second gift. "Peanut butter?"

"For Buddy. There's a related—"

A black and white streak shot across the room as Kyle held up the hollow purple ball.

"It'll keep him occupied while we use the last gift," she whispered, suddenly nervous.

He gave her a curious look and slid the tin out of the bag. "Altoids?"

She grinned. Fake it till you make it. "You bet. Leave the Red Bull here and follow me."

She swirled past him, letting her fingers trail across his lower abdomen as she stepped toward the living area. Her coat hit the floor, followed by her top, and she turned in the middle of the room, wearing yoga pants and a black bra. Kyle paced toward her, heat rolling off him. As he reached her, she sank to her knees and parted her lips. "May I have a mint, sir?"

Kyle groaned and opened the package. She stuck her tongue out to accept the candy he offered, drawing it into her mouth. He held onto it for a minute, feeling the warmth of her mouth around his fingers, then he slipped them out and swiped her lower lip with the pad of his thumb. "Your mouth looks so damn good glistening wet like that."

Laney smirked and fluttered her eyelashes. "You say the nicest things," she murmured, tugging at his belt buckle. She was eager to have him in her mouth, a curious fact that she didn't want to explore right at that moment. Or ever. She breathed in and out, steadying her nerves.

———

KYLE GROANED as Laney slipped her hand into his open jeans and wrapped her cool fingers around his straining cock. His ass flexed on its own when she slid her hand up and down the shaft, and he barely kept his hips from thrusting into her face. He had loved her mouth on him the other day, and wanted more. He stroked her hair, resisting the urge to wrap his fist around her ponytail. "I can't wait to be inside you," he said with a growl.

She shook her head. "This isn't a prelude to anything. I saw that tin and all I could think of was making you finish in my mouth."

He twitched against her hand. That was the only part of him that wasn't speechless.

"I've never done that with anyone, you know."

That low confession tore him to pieces. For all her bravado, Laney was still that same sweet girl he used to know, and he wasn't sure they were doing the right thing, in this moment or in general. Worse than that was he didn't care enough to stop. Her pink lips parted in anticipation and he stroked her cheek, first with his fingers, then more firmly with his thumb, encouraging her to open. Her eyes widened for a second, and he worried he was being too crude, but then they sparked with wicked delight, and she darted her tongue out and around the head of his shaft.

She didn't take him into her mouth right away, and while he couldn't contain the odd groan or cock twitch, he let her set the pace. This was her gift, and he appreciated any variation she might offer. She licked, breathed, and nuzzled his sex. She wasn't teasing or playing a game. She was exploring his body, figuring out exactly what he liked. It was a level of intimacy he'd only ever had with her, and as he stared down at this amazing, one-of-a-kind woman, he feared he might never find it again.

She pushed his hands into her hair, encouraging him to show her what pace he wanted as she took more of his length into her mouth, and any worry was pushed out of his brain as she swirled her magic minty tongue along his shaft. It was hot and cold at the same time, and he couldn't stop his hips from jerking forward. His eyes rolled back in his head and he gave himself over to the soft, rocking sensations. The coordination of hand and mouth was tentative at first, then bolder. She wobbled her head back and forth, in an alternating pattern to her soft hand sliding around the base of him. *Jesus.* She was hitting all of his buttons, particularly one big button on the underside of his swollen head—which, goddamn it, her tongue just swirled over. He jerked his hips and she hummed her pride around his cock. He pried his eyes open and gazed down at her. *Shit, she looks so fucking pleased with herself.* As she should.

"I'm close, sweet—uhhhhhh—so close..."

She maintained a steady rhythm, her cheeks hollowing ever so slightly as she worked him toward his release. He was afraid his knees might buckle, but she shook her head when he tapped her shoulder. She wanted this, and heaven help him, so did he, even if it felled him.

"Fuuuu—uhhhh—Laney. Oh. Here it comes. Fuck!" He exploded in her mouth, and all around her, his body crumpling forward, and oh yeah, there went his knees. She eased him to the floor in front of her and he wove his fingers into her hair, burying her face in his heaving chest. He was dazed, overwhelmed in the aftermath of a spectacular blow job. He should probably tell her just how good it was, although his physical reaction pretty much gave that away. "Wow. I knew I liked your mouth, but...wow."

She climbed into his lap, careful to avoid pressing on his well-used centre. She glowed with satisfaction. "That was fun."

"Yeah?"

She nodded.

"Give me a minute, and I'm going to return the favour."

"Oh, no. You don't have—"

"Okay, first of all? I want to. Want. To. More than you can know."

A notched eyebrow made him laugh. "Okay, maybe you know. Making you come undone..." he mouthed the side of her neck, "...watching you climax..." he moved to the pulse point at the base of her neck as she shivered, "...licking you into unconsciousness—"

"Hey, what?" Laney pulled herself up tall, as tall as she could get while sitting on a half-naked man. "That sounds more traumatizing than hot."

"Crap, and I was on a roll. Pass me an Altoid and I'll put my tongue to better use." He waggled his eyebrow at her and she laughed, but then he growled and she leapt for the tin.

10

Laney rolled to her feet and grabbed her yoga pants. "That was spectacular. We're going to have to do that again before I head back to Chicago."

She turned away from Kyle as he pushed himself up off the floor, busying herself with getting dressed and straightening her ponytail. She hated the nasty tug in her gut that told her she wanted more than one more time, that she hoped he might take that road trip next summer because she'd never get enough of him.

She hated she hadn't seen it coming. It wasn't love, but it was addictive, and that was too dangerous to be let loose. So by saying one more time she was just establishing boundaries, for both their sakes.

Kyle didn't blink. "How about Boxing Day? When are you leaving? I'm busy tomorrow but yeah, I want to do that again." He pulled her back against his chest and covered her abdomen with his big warm hands. "Maybe at the same time. And then I want to bury myself inside you." He lowered his voice and brought his lips to her ear. "I love the feel of you wrapped around my cock. You're so hot and tight. A perfect fit."

She shivered at the image, wanting Kyle on top of her right there. "No fair, I have to go."

Was it rude to suggest sneaking away from their families on Christmas Day for a hookup? Probably.

Definitely. Get a grip, Laney, you can go two more days without sex with Kyle. Good practice for the rest of your life.

"Yes, Boxing Day. I'll come over. I think Evie's taking the kids to Dale's place for the day. And then … I'm probably leaving the day after that." It was a little white lie, she wasn't planning on leaving until the 30th, but things could change.

Kyle squeezed and she could feel him press his face into her hair. "Then let's make our last time together a good one."

———

WHEN TWO DAYS had gone by without hearing from Laney after her first visit to his house, Kyle had convinced himself that she just wanted to sleep with him once for closure. The possibility of not tasting her again pained him, but he needed to accept what she was willing to offer on her terms. But now she'd stopped by again. On Christmas Eve. He couldn't help but hope that meant something. Because he wanted more. A lot more. The sex was off-the-charts, and if she'd be open to it, hell yes he'd drive to Chicago for a booty call. Probably more than once. He wasn't stupid enough to think Laney would ever open her heart to him again, but he'd tried searching for love elsewhere and failed miserably. *And broken yet another heart in the process.* He was done hoping he might find his everything in another person, but he'd stumbled into something spectacular with Laney again. Something would have to be enough, and if he had anything to say about it, Boxing Day wouldn't be the last time they were together.

His ringing cell phone snapped his attention back to the moment at hand. He glanced down the low reclaimed wood coffee table beside him and saw his niece's photo on the call display.

"Do you need to get that? I can let myself out." She was fully dressed again, a lingering warmth in her cheeks the only evidence that they had just devoured each other.

Kyle shook his head. "It's my brother, I'll call him once you go. Probably just wants me to pick stuff up on my way to my parents' farm."

"If you stop at the grocery store, be prepared for the third degree by Karen Miller."

"Oh god, I'm sorry. Did you see her this morning? She likes to gossip, but she means well."

She shrugged. "Yeah, I think she's trying to be a good friend to you. I'll be honest, I prefer the anonymity of the big city, but it can't be said that people don't care here. I also got asked if I'd seen you by a few people at the coffee shop."

Kyle grabbed her coat off the floor and held it out for her. "Again, I'm sorry."

"I don't see what you have to be sorry about. It's the nature of small towns."

"It's more than that," Kyle shifted back on his heels. "My break up with Crystal was pretty public."

She turned, her lips pursed.

"She, uh…she had the idea that I was still hung up on you."

"And everyone in town knows this?"

He nodded, two awkward little jerks of the head, his gaze drifting over her shoulder.

Laney zipped her coat up and moved closer to the fridge, looking at the family photo taken at his parents' farm. Crystal was partially covered by more recent candids of his niece and nephew. She peeled back one of the pictures to get a better look. His arm was wrapped around Crystal's waist and she was leaning into his side.

"You look like a serious couple here."

"We were. We lived together for a year."

"What happened?"

"We broke up."

"Why?"

Kyle didn't want to answer that question.

She turned, levelling a far too insightful gaze at him. "When did you break up exactly?"

"Two years ago."

"At Christmas?"

"In November."

"Around my dad's funeral."

His heart was pounding in his chest. This wasn't how this conversation was supposed to go. "Yes, but…"

"What happened?"

"I'm not hung up on you. I promise you that. There's a part of me that will always love the Laney I used to date, and I obviously like the Laney that you've become, but I'm not confused about what's possible and what's not."

"What happened?" She didn't look mad, but she was guarded in a way he hadn't seen since she'd first come over the other day. Giggling, teasing Laney had left the building.

He took a deep breath. "The night of the funeral. I got drunk after I saw you. I don't really do that anymore. I had a few wild years after you left, and then I put that behind me. So Crystal had never seen me blitzed. She didn't like it. And I was rambling on about how I should have seized the opportunity to talk to you, tell you that I forgave you for leaving—"

"Excuse me?" She flared with anger and he reached out to calm her.

"—which I realize now is ridiculous and all on me, I promise. But I was rambling, and then we were fighting. We never fought. We had a simple, easy life together, and then in one big bang it was over. I don't even remember exactly what was said, but I slept on the couch and the next day she boxed up everything I owned and kicked me out."

"This is all just … too weird. And why am I involved exactly?"

"You're the golden girl of Wardham, didn't you know that? The fancy doctor." He grinned, hoping that she'd take his teasing as an olive branch. "The town took that opportunity to rehash how I broke your heart. I got a bit defensive at first, I admit, but then I realized they were right."

"I had no idea. My mom...my sister...they didn't say anything. I would have thought everyone would have forgotten about me."

He took a chance and stepped forward to pull her against his chest. "Impossible to forget you, Laney." He kissed her head. "Now, you have to go before your mother figures out what we've been doing. Please tell me that you're still coming over on Boxing Day."

She took her time responding. She squeezed her lips together and opened the front door. Backlit by sunlight, all he could see was wisps of blond hair and a face in shadow. Kyle felt an unexpected pressure in his chest. He should have come clean fully the other day, instead of letting his dick take over.

"This would be a lot for anyone to deal with," she said in a quick breath. "Luckily I think emotions are overrated. And you're fantastic in the sack, so yeah, you'll see me again."

And with that she was gone. Kyle thought he heard a little giggle as the door clicked shut, but it was probably wishful thinking.

———

THE FARMHOUSE WAS empty when Laney returned, a small miracle for which she would be eternally thankful. Evie had propped a note next to the kettle, explaining that she had taken the boys sledding, and they'd be home at noon. She glanced at the clock and decided to put some soup on for lunch, a gesture that was much appreciated when two frosty little boys bustled in twenty minutes later.

"Isn't Mom with you?"

Evie shook her head. "She popped over to Ted's with some cookies. I thought she'd be back by now."

Laney notched one eyebrow at her sister, who rolled her eyes.

"What? It's possible. It's been two years. I'm not saying they're in love, but she's a beautiful woman with lots of life still to live."

"Bite your tongue, Laney. Besides, I think there were a bunch of them meeting over there."

"Them?"

"There's an informal group of older single people, they play bridge and gossip."

"Hot stuff."

Evie laughed. "Don't make fun, we're not far off from that ourselves."

It was Laney's turn to roll her eyes now, and without thinking, she said, "I can think of a number of better things to do with a willing and able man."

Evie shot her sons a quick glance, but they were absorbed in debate about the best Transformer. "Do any of them at Kyle's place today?"

"Evie!" She felt the heat flood up her chest and spread across her face. So much for not caring if she was caught. "Uhhhh. I stopped there. To talk."

"Is that why you just turned purple? It's not the best look for you, you're too fair to pull it off." Evie leapt out of swiping range as Laney lunged at her. "It's okay, little sister, rumour has it that you're a trained medical professional, I'm sure whatever you did was entirely clinical."

She groaned and buried her face in her hands. "Don't tell Mom. Please. It's...I don't know. It's a fling, it's something we just need to get out of our systems. I'm not deluding myself into thinking it's anything else."

Evie waved in the air, abandoning the conversation. "Okay, mum's the word. I think you're playing with fire, but maybe you need to get burned."

Claire returned from across the road shortly after lunch, carrying a tin of all butter shortbread courtesy of one of the bridge players, which Laney happily dug into while thumbing her nose at her sister.

"You two are worse than Connor and Max, seriously. Now, what should we do this afternoon? Puzzles? Charades? Monopoly?"

The boys started hopping in excitement at the last option, so Claire and Laney joined them in a rousing competition of real estate development while Evie busied herself in the kitchen, popping in occasionally to capture some of the tenser moments on video. By four o'clock, it was obvious that Connor was going to slowly bleed them all dry with his hotel resort complex on Boardwalk and Park Place, and before Max threw a low-blood sugar induced hissy fit about losing, Claire suggested that they call it a game and get cleaned up for dinner.

Max immediately protested having to put on fancy clothes, a campaign Connor could support with ease, so while the boys pled their case to the unswaying judges of holiday decorum, their mother and grandmother, Laney snuck away to grab the first shower. Scrubbed clean, she considered the two holiday outfits laid out on her bed: a dark green jersey dress with long sleeves and a cowl neck, and black pants and a sparkly red top. She had planned to wear the red top for Christmas morning, to go with an elf hat that she picked up, but the growing darkness prompted her to grab the pants. The hat would go just as nicely with the dress, and she would be less likely to be asked to sit on the floor and play with the boys in the morning when they are absorbed in their new toys.

She was the first back downstairs, so she pulled the bread pudding from the oven and lit the candles in the center of the table. Next down the stairs were Connor and Max, in matching buttoned down white shirts and knit vests with contrasting Argyll patterns on the chest. Grandma and Mom had obviously compromised with the boys, as they both still wore jeans, and Laney's heart squeezed. In front of her stood two little men.

"You look beautiful, Aunt Laney," Max said, and the squeezing turned into a full on bittersweet ache.

"And you both look dashing. Wasn't it a good idea to dress up after all?"

"I guess so," Connor said. "As long as we don't have to do it every day."

She laughed. "I agree."

Evie and Claire soon joined them and they settled in around the oversized kitchen table. Claire lifted her wine glass, and the others followed suit. Connor and Max had goblets as well, filled with ginger ale, and they grinned proudly as their grandmother began her toast. "Our lives have changed a lot over the last two years, and that has been challenging, but tonight I am just...happy. I'm so happy to have both of my daughters home for the holidays. I'm blessed with good health and the ability to keep up my amazing grandsons. Connor and Max, you keep me young!"

"Really? I think they're aging me at a stupendous rate," Evie muttered, but the happy tear in her eye betrayed her words, and the boys squeezed her from either side.

"It has been a year of stepping back into the world," Claire continued, her words slowing as she considered what to say next. "And I hope that I'm setting a good example for all of you. Evie and Laney, you have both always been fearless, have followed your dreams, and I want that to always be true. You have far exceeded anything your dad and I ever did. He would be so proud of both of you."

Laney looked across the table at her sister. Evie was the textbook definition of fearless, barely stumbling after her separation. Laney didn't feel nearly that brave, just lucky in her career and not much else. She swallowed hard, trying to get rid of the lump in her throat, not sure what to say. Her gazed slipped over to her mother, who beamed at her with overwhelming love and understanding. A tentative smile crawled up her cheeks. "Thanks, Mom. That was really sweet. I hope..."

"I know, sweetie. We're all our own worst enemies. Trust yourself."

AFTER SECOND HELPINGS of bread pudding, Laney and the boys settled on the couch to watch *A Christmas Story* before bed while Evie and Claire tidied up the kitchen. Connor suggested they also track Santa on the NORAD website, so the movie was interrupted every few minutes by Max poking Laney's side, urging her to refresh the screen.

When Santa moved across the Atlantic Ocean, Connor and Max scrambled up the stairs and brushed their teeth without being asked. Evie joined them as they tucked into their beds, and Laney left her sister in charge of bedtime stories.

The bottle of champagne had been chilling in the fridge since she arrived. She set it on a tray. It wasn't likely that her mom would have flutes, but Laney pulled a chair over to the cabinets to take a quick look just in case. Her parents had renovated the kitchen when Laney was in college, and her mother had insisted on extra tall upper cabinets. The extra storage shelves at the top housed large serving platters and soup tureens. If fancy wine glasses existed anywhere in the farmhouse, that's where she would find them.

She found the smooth black pressed cardboard box hiding behind a set of googly-eyes hardboiled egg cups. She'd forgotten about the pair of crystal flutes. They were a wedding gift to her parents from a family friend, and she'd often seen them pull the box out on their anniversary when she was younger. She didn't want to add any unnecessary melancholy to the holidays, but her gut told her that they would only bring happiness to the evening.

"Goodness, Laney, be careful up there."

"You shouldn't have built such high cupboards, it's your own fault." Laney turned and grinned at her mother. To reach the top shelf, she'd climbed up on to the counter, and that never went over well with parents. "I found your wedding champagne flutes, can we use them tonight?"

"Of course, pass them down to me. There's only two … let me

see if I can find a third wine glass that would work." Claire set the box on the table and moved across the room to the china display. "Here!"

Laney slid to the floor and took the spare glass flute from her mother. Much lighter than the others, it was embossed with the name of a local winery.

"Your dad and I went to a class about sparkling wine at Water's Edge. You know how your dad was about wine, it was never his thing, but he surprised me with the tickets." Claire's voice was soft with memory. "That was just six months before he died. He wasn't much of a romantic, you know, but then he would do something like that and blow my socks off."

Laney inspected the wine glass with new appreciation. "Way to go, Dad! And it's kind of cool that they gave you a souvenir to take home."

Claire's eyes, bright with happy tears, crinkled into silent laughter. "Oh no," she gasped. "Your dad stole that for me. We got a bit tipsy, you see, and I told him that it was one of the best nights of my life. We had…I hope this isn't too much information, but it really felt like we had been flirting all night. And the wine was really quite good. It was a heady combination. At the end of the night your dad pushed me against the bar and kissed me, and apparently, he took that opportunity to slide his glass into my purse."

Laney stared at her mother, mouth agape. She didn't know what shocked her more, her parents making out or engaging in petty theft.

"Don't look so horrified, Delaney." Claire slipped back into her usual prim personality.

"I'm not, I promise. I think I'm impressed, actually. Up against the bar, eh? That's hot." This time laughter washed over and through them both, and that's how Evie found them, hugging in the kitchen, tears of joy streaming down their faces.

Claire kept the souvenir glass for herself and the girls each took a crystal flute. Laney popped the cork and as the golden effervescence overflowed, they giggled and cheered. They settled in front of the Christmas tree and the twinkling coloured lights bounced off their drinks, a dazzling backdrop for a special announcement. Not that Laney wanted to do make a big deal about it, but she'd made a decision that she hoped Evie would understand and appreciate.

"Evie, do you know how impressed I am with how you've handled the divorce? Starting your own business, putting up with Mom—" Claire poked Laney in the ribs for that one "—and having energy to run around with the boys every day?"

Evie raised her eyebrows, looking unsure as to where the conversation was going, but she couldn't keep a smile off her face. "Keep going. Champagne and compliments, a girl could get used to this."

"I know that you don't need anything."

Evie winked. "Mmmm, I wouldn't say that. I wouldn't say no to a pool boy."

"Okay." Laney laughed. "I'll put in an order for one. But seriously, even though I know you don't need it, I want to do something for the boys. Set up an education account."

Evie sat up. She didn't say anything, but Laney could tell she was considering how to say no.

"Don't say no. Please. I'm not offering this because I feel guilty for not being here, or because I think that you need any help. It's just that I have the means, and they're so smart, it would be nice if when they get to university, money isn't a factor."

Laney had incurred significant student loans, because their parents hadn't been able to help much past her first degree. She was paying that debt off at an accelerated rate now that she was fully trained, and it would soon be gone, giving her financial freedom.

Claire touched her back. "Something like that would have made a big difference for you, wouldn't it have?"

Laney shook her head. "Mom, that's never been a thought for me, I promise. I'm lucky that I'm going to be debt free soon, but there are many graduate school tracks that don't lead to my level of income, and if Connor or Max ever want to study art or animal migration or whatever, I hope they graduate in the clear."

Evie still hadn't said anything, but she nodded silently, swiping away tears. Laney crawled over to her sister and cuddled into her side. "We're family. What's mine is yours."

Evie pressed her cheek into the top of Laney's head and swallowed hard. "Thank you. You mean it?"

She nodded.

"Excellent. You can take the boys home with you." And once again, the Calhoun women laughed.

11

———

The thunder of children's footsteps on the stairs woke Laney up, and she hurried to the landing just as Connor and Max discovered their full stockings hanging from the banister into the hallway on the first floor. They glanced up at her, bright faces thrilled that the promise of a magical visit had actually happened. Behind her, Evie bounced, barely able to contain her own excitement. Claire mumbled something about coffee and scones as she slipped past them, but Laney and her sister were happy to watch the boys hoot and holler about the action figures, magazines, chocolate, personalized mixed CDs, and even socks and oranges that Santa had left them.

"Can we open our presents too, Mom?" Max peered up between the balusters. Evie shook her head and his face sank into a pout.

"Max, remember what we talked about last night. Mommy needs coffee and a bite to eat, and she needs to get the video camera ready. Then you can open your presents. It won't be long, I promise. Go see how Grandma is doing with first breakfast."

Connor's stomach growled at the mention of food, so Max followed his brother down the hall. First and second breakfasts were a long standing Calhoun Christmas tradition. Second breakfast was really an early lunch, not usually hitting the table until eleven in the morning or later, but it was always breakfast food. Orange juice, some fancy egg dish, sausage, toast, fried tomatoes. First breakfast was something quick to keep everyone sustained through present opening and playing.

Claire tasked Connor with carrying the tray, loaded with scones, clotted cream, preserves, and glasses of milk for the boys. Max followed with plates and cutlery, and Claire brought up the rear with three steaming mugs of coffee. Evie gave the official nod to Max, and as the women dug into the food as wrapping paper and ribbons started flying through the air.

Max insisted on sorting the presents by matching wrapping paper, so first they opened the gifts Evie had wrapped, then Claire's, and finally the boxes that Laney had brought from Chicago. Her gifts for the boys had been suggested by Evie: a tablet for Connor and a Nintendo DS for Max. It had been harder to find the right presents for her mother and sister, but she'd finally found items that were special enough. An oversized black cashmere wrap for her mother, with a hardcover bestseller that hid the author's signature inside the front cover nestled on top. She'd stood in line for an hour at the DePaul Center Barnes & Noble to get that personalized note, *For Claire, who never gives up,* and it was worth it to see her mother get all verklempt with happy tears. For Evie, she'd gone hog-wild in Sephora, filling a gift basket with treats from Smashbox, Bobbi Brown, Philosophy and Urban Decay.

She had been spoiled herself that morning, with her family giving her new workout clothes, gift certificates for her favourite Chicago takeout restaurants, a desk calendar featuring pictures of the boys, a pile of fantasy novels by her favourite authors, a sparkly stethoscope decoration handmade by Max and a stocking full of dark chocolate and Lush bath bombs. And wrapped in and around all of the gift giving was a happy warmth, a joy and grounded appreciation that they were able to spend the holidays together.

Two hours later, Max had convinced Connor to set aside his tablet to stage an attack on the castle (which Max would easily fend off, as he kept the superior fire power tools for his own force), and Claire was prepping for second breakfast. Laney had gotten dressed in her green jersey dress and thigh-high grey knit socks, her new favourite winter leg covering. All the warmth of tights without the annoying rolling waistband. She finished the outfit with the green and white elf hat, and did little jig at her reflection in the mirror.

"You're happy." Evie strolled into Laney's room.

"It's Christmas."

"Mm-hmm. Are you expecting a visitor today?"

"What, Kyle?" Laney shook her head. "He's got family stuff today. I am going to see him tomorrow, though. Keep that under your hat, okay?"

Evie smirked.

"What?"

"I'm not sure it's going to be a secret for long. Kyle's downstairs in the kitchen having coffee with Mom."

"EVIE!" She spun around in a circle, looking for something that she couldn't remember all of a sudden, then gave up and glared at her sister. "I'm going downstairs. You. Be. Good."

"Always, always," Evie said, chuckling under her breath.

Laney managed to slow her pace, if not her heart rate, as she went downstairs and she strolled into the kitchen with relative calm. "Hey, you." She looked back and forth between Kyle and her mom. "You are…here. Having coffee. That's nice."

Kyle smiled. "Yep. Just being neighbourly."

Claire stood up to make room for Laney at the table, but Kyle waved her down.

"Actually, Claire, I was hoping that Laney might go for a quick walk with me."

All three Calhoun women nodded, each in a different way, and Laney kicked her sister in the shin for no good reason other than they were sisters and she was off-kilter. Evie giggled and instead of kicking her back, gave her a gentle shove toward the door. She slid into her boots, pulled on her parka and followed Kyle outside.

"I like your hat." Kyle flicked the furry white brim. "Festive."

Laney stared at him. "What are you doing here? I mean, thank you. But what are you doing here? This really isn't a good idea."

Kyle shrugged. "I didn't think it would be that big a deal. I'm just heading home to change. I spent the night at my parents' place, but there are twelve people competing for the shower, so this is easier. And it was a good excuse to bring you a present." He leaned in close to whisper in her ear. "Because I really, really liked your present, and you deserve something in return."

She had started the slow burn of arousal the second Evie told her Kyle was downstairs, but that brush of hot breath against her ear sent her up in flames. She sucked in a breath, mindful that they were still in view of the kitchen windows. He pulled her toward his truck, and she had to skip to keep up. Excited in more ways than one, she pressed her hip into his as they stopped next to the driver's side door.

"Down, girl," Kyle murmured.

"You don't understand what you do to me." She groaned into his shoulder. "It has literally been years since I've been this turned on, and I only have a couple of days to take advantage of it. This is a bonus that I wasn't counting on."

Kyle turned his back against the truck and tugged Laney hard between his legs. He stared at her for a beat, and then opened and closed his mouth. His beautiful mouth, that could go from an open, happy grin to hungry, restless kissing in the blink of an eye. But he wasn't leaning in to kiss her, and he wasn't grinning. He raked his eyes over her face, a tiny twitch in his jaw the only betrayal of an otherwise neutral facade. She had no idea what he was feeling, or thinking, and she hoped that this wasn't about to get heavy. Hot and heavy, on the other hand, would be just fine.

"I was going to give you your present and a quick kiss and be on my way," Kyle said, drawing out each word with deliberate calm. "But when you say things like that, when you remind me that the next time that we're together might be the last time, then I can't help but want to drag you off to a dark corner. You make me lose my mind, Laney."

She let a happy smile creep across her face. She didn't need to play the seductress, or any other game. They wanted each other with honest abandon, and neither of them would fight it.

"Want to go make out in the barn?"

Kyle lowered his face to hers, rubbing their noses together. "Abso-fucking-lutely. But first—" he opened the truck door and grabbed a slightly crumbled, probably re-used, glittery red gift bag. "This is for you."

She reached inside and pulled out a familiar well-worn t-shirt. "Your swim team shirt?"

"You used to like sleeping in it."

She nodded, remembering. "It looks exactly the same."

Kyle returned the shirt to the gift bag and stashed it in the truck, then captured her hand in his, pulling Laney toward the barn. "I haven't worn it since we broke up. I actually tucked it away in a box, which has lived at my parents' place for a while now. I was thinking about you last night, and decided it might be a fitting Christmas present."

Appreciation fluttered through Laney's lower belly, softening the tug of arousal into something infinitely more dangerous. She needed to be careful that they didn't conflate whatever they were doing now with what they used to have. She knew that Kyle didn't mean for that shirt to be a Trojan horse, and she understood why he would think it was the most appropriate gift—it was free, and sexy in a not-trying-too-hard kind of way. And he didn't need to get her anything at all, but now that he had, it felt right. Dangerous, but right.

"You're thinking hard about something." Kyle pulled her close.

She shook her head. "Nothing important, don't worry. Thank you, for the shirt, and the visit. And the last few days. You are...you are just so easy to like. How did I forget that about you?"

"It's been a long time." Kyle shrugged. "Don't overthink it. This is just us having fun, right?"

"Right." But even as relief flooded into her heart, Laney wasn't so sure that either of them was being totally honest on that point.

KYLE JUST WANTED her to stop thinking. Giving her the t-shirt was risky, but she accepted it as he intended. There were never any hidden agendas with Laney, something he appreciated even more after living with Crystal. There weren't any promises of a future life together, either, but he didn't need to live like a monk anymore. Two years was more than enough time for soul-searching and penance. As long as Laney was close enough to touch, to breathe in, to taste like his goddamn last meal, he would take whatever she offered and not ask any questions about what it might cost him when she inevitably left.

The neatly painted red and white barn was built on a slope, running away from the house, so the closest door opened into the top floor. Kyle knew that Claire had sold her herd of sheep after her husband passed away, and leased her fields to neighbours for crops, but he didn't know what she had stored in the barn. Stepping inside, he was surprised to see a speedboat on a trailer bed.

"Mom said there was a boat in here, but I thought she meant a canoe or a rowboat." Laney whistled, walking around to take in the length of it. "Want to get in?"

Kyle grinned and offered her a hand as she jumped up on the trailer. "You going to be okay in that dress?"

She winked. "You might need to give me a little boost."

He joined her on the trailer, close enough to feel her breath warm his face as she looked up at him. "Hold on tight," he whispered, cupping her waist in his hands. She was feather light, the warmth of her slim frame and her fragile scent more of a strain than the effort it would take to lift her. With a quick count to three, he had Laney up and scootched back so she was sitting on the edge of the boat, her knees at his chest.

"Do you like my tights?"

He slid his hands down her calves and into the top of her sheepskin boots, admiring the narrow ankles and subtle curves more than what covered them, but he knew how to answer this question. "They're keeping some of my favourite parts nice and warm."

"Not all of your favourite parts," Laney said with a wicked smile, lifting her skirt just high enough to extend an invitation.

Kyle curved his fingers up over her knees, across the tops of her thighs until he found a knit edge and the soft, smooth skin above. He sucked in a quick breath as his brain translated to his cock. Warm. Open. Inviting. He splayed his hands wide, his wrists on the elastic top of the sock stockings, the tips of his fingers grazing the lace edge of her panties. "These are the best tights ever," he said, his voice rough with intent. "Lean back."

She shook her head and reached down to toy with his belt buckle, pressing her breasts into his face in the process. "Come on up here and I'll hop on for a ride."

Kyle stilled her hands and smacked her lightly on the hip. "Sorry, sweetheart. I really wasn't planning on this. I don't have a condom."

She groaned and pressed her forehead against his. He could practically hear her thought process and he needed to put a stop to it. *Way too tempting*. His cock twitched and his heart rate picked up. He was a bastard for even considering it.

"Kyle," she whispered. "I have an IUD. I know it's stupid, but..."

"That should be the end of the sentence, Doctor." She bit her lip, then his ear, and it was his turn to waver. Definitely a bastard. "I haven't been with anyone in two years. Had a full check up in the summer."

"This would be my first time ever without a condom. I know

it's reckless, but I trust you." She brushed her lips against his. "Be inside me. Please."

He held her face against his, deepening the kiss. She tasted like berry jam. He was going to hell, and she tasted like goddamn fruit. With a ragged breath, he gave her a little push to move into the boat.

"Besides, it's cold." She swung her legs into the boat and, after pausing to divest herself of her underwear, she moved over, making room for him to join her on the bench seat. "This way we can share body heat."

He was more than ready, and he knew that Laney would be too, so Kyle pulled her into his lap and under the warm cover that her dress provided, he unzipped and fisted his erection toward home. *Don't get carried away. Maybe an amazing five star resort. Better than home, but you can't stay forever.* She was slick, and her folds parted readily for him. He didn't enter her right away, wanting to steal a moment of anticipation, and she twisted her hips trying to capture the head of his cock. He chuckled and reached between them to stroke around her clit, earning a whimper of appreciation. Her hips jerked wildly, achieving what her deliberate wiggling only teased at. *Home.*

She was tight, hot, and impossibly soft. He was gripped in a velvet sleeve lined in the most addictive substance known to man, and as Kyle drove his hips up and into her he knew he'd never get enough of Laney. He needed to deal with that thought, but this wasn't the time, not when he was half out of his mind, lunging toward a hard orgasm, desperate to take her with him, make it good—no, amazing—for her so he'd get to do this again. Over and over they ground against each other, her fingers replacing his as she climbed the peak. And then she was clenching him, her pussy spasming around his cock, her hands in a death grip on his shoulders, her thighs tight around his hips, and he jerked too, coming inside her.

They clung to each other for a long moment as their breathing returned to normal. He couldn't get over how simple and easy this still was between them. No, scratch that. This was its own thing. There was no comparing it to the past. "That was unbelievable. Fast, but wow. You felt amazing, Laney."

She rewarded his compliment with an uncharacteristic blush that tugged at his gut, reminding him again that she wasn't as worldly as she played at. "Better tuck yourself away before I get up, wouldn't want my favourite part of you to get cold." And just like that, she was back to business.

At his the truck, Kyle squeezed her hand and gave her quick, hard kiss that left her lips numb and her heart racing. "I'll make dinner tomorrow night. Come over around six. And Laney … I'd like you to stay for the entire evening. I want more than a stolen moment."

12

---

oxing Day started with Pilates, Evie pushing them extra hard because of the bread pudding. Laney was still waiting for her mother and sister to say something, anything, about Kyle's visit. She hadn't told them that she was going out that night, and once the boys disappeared to build a Lego fortress, she bit the bullet.

"So about Kyle's visit yesterday," she started, rolling her exercise mat up to keep her hands busy. "He stopped by to invite me over for dinner. To catch up. Tonight. And I'm going."

Evie raised both eyebrows, as if to say, *riiiiigghhhht*, but she kept her lips shut and for that, Laney was grateful. Claire just nodded sagely, as if this had been her grand plan all along, but she too kept her silence.

"I'm sure I'm going to regret asking, but you seriously don't have any questions?"

"Oh Laney, I have a million questions," said Claire. "But asking them won't change anything and I'm not sure you have the answers yet. I'd think you must be nervous?"

She wasn't. She considered Kyle's question from the day before. *More of a command then a question.* The directness of what he had said surprised her, and she hadn't answered right away.

Instead she unzipped his fleece sweater and pressed her face into his neck, feeling the warmth transfer from his skin to hers. It was a reasonable request, one that he wouldn't have to ask of any other date. But it was more than she'd ordinarily give of herself, and Laney didn't care. She'd leaned fully against the wide, hard planes of his chest, acknowledging that she did want more. And there was no reason to hold back when they only had a few days. They should embrace the possibilities of a fling, the freedom of zero expectations. She'd nodded her head against his body and then turned without a word and fled inside before she said something smart-alecky that might ruin the moment.

"Why would I be nervous?"

Evie and Claire exchanged silent looks.

"Hello? Evie, what's Mom alluding to?"

Her sister shrugged. "Oh, you know. Kyle's always loved you, he's the only man you've ever loved, yadda yadda yadda. Potential for great messiness. That kind of thing."

Laney sighed and plunked her butt down on the couch next to her mother. "I promise you, Kyle and I are on the same page about that. We both want to move forward in our lives. And we want very different things. No one is going to get hurt."

Claire cocked her head to the side. "Just how much have you two been talking? That's some pretty heavy subject matter."

"I know, I'm just as surprised as you. I wasn't going to go there, but he told me a bit about his ex and how he's been stuck in a bit of a loop. I have too, in a way, so it was cathartic to compare ruts." Laney didn't know how much she wanted to share with her mother and sister, but they had each been through so much more than her, that she didn't feel right blowing them off once again as if they didn't get it. They did, absolutely. "There was a guy that I was seeing. I broke up with him just before coming home. I wasn't as nice to him as I should have been. I've just gotten so good at guarding myself that I didn't notice when I went from being careful to actually using other people. So running into Kyle, and admitting that I had some unresolved issues there…it opened me up to other possibilities."

Claire looked piqued, her mind obviously whirling between the possibility of more grandchildren and the likelihood of a once-again broken-hearted daughter.

"Not with Kyle, Mom. And not necessarily love, but just honest connections with people. I'm really looking forward to having dinner with an old friend tonight, and it's been way too long since I've said that. I just need to meet some new Kyles in Chicago."

Evie had been quietly putting away Pilates gear, listening with one ear but trying not to react in her usual big sister way. Laney looked up at her, giving her an official opportunity to comment. Evie nodded and smiled. "Hell, I'd like to meet some new Kyles here, too. I get it."

"So…why not with Kyle, then?"

Laney sighed. "God, Mom, you're giving me whiplash. There's too much history. We live in different cities—different countries! We have divergent life goals. Why on earth would you want me to be with him?"

"Because he obviously makes you happy."

And damned if that wasn't the wildcard of truth. Laney shook her head. "That's the worst reason I could think of." She squeezed her mother's hand and stood up, wanting to avoid the concern she would find on Claire's face. "I let my happiness be wrapped up in Kyle once before. Never again. Not him, or anyone else."

———

KYLE'S HOUSE smelled like oranges and wood fire. She stepped inside, shrugging off her winter coat, and made an appreciative sound that was rewarded with a quick hug and a kiss on the top of her head.

"Your place is pretty cozy for a construction site." Laney kicked her boots to the black plastic tray next to the door and wandered into the living room. On the ottoman, a large three-wick candle flickered, bouncing waves of light off the shiny glass tray underneath it. Another tray had been placed on the rug in front of the wood stove, this one holding a bottle of red wine and two glasses. "Why, Kyle Nixon, are you looking to get lucky tonight?"

She turned and gave him an appraising look, which only lasted a few seconds before they both burst into laughter. Lips still twitching, Kyle waved her toward the couch and poured two glasses of wine. "I'm not looking for anything other than to be a good host, Laney Calhoun."

"Liar, liar, pants on fire," she murmured, lifting the glass to her lips. After taking a sip, she tucked her feet under her bum and leaned back against the couch. "Where's Buddy?"

"I took him to my parents' farm for the night. He's not exactly conducive to romance."

"You didn't need to—"

He shook his head. "I did it for me. I wanted you all to myself tonight."

Oh. "I like Buddy."

"I know." Kyle stood a few feet away, arms crossed, an inscrutable look on his face.

Under his gaze, her skin felt hot and hypersensitive. "Stop staring at me. Do you need any help with dinner? It smells great."

He smirked, then moved to the other end of the couch, sitting far enough away to give her personal space. His eyes, on the other hand, never left her face, and she blushed.

"So…this is really good wine."

"I'm glad you like it. Do you remember Tyler West? He bought a defunct winery a few years ago and turned the business around with his brother's help. This is their first widely distributed vintage."

Her eyes widened. "Do you mean Go West Winery? That's your friend Ty? Wow. Good for him. I read an article about the company a few months ago, but didn't connect the name. It mentioned someone else, I thought."

He nodded. "Probably Evan. He's more the face of the company. Ty's all about the grapes and the production process."

"I admire that entrepreneurial spirit. I don't even have the courage to open my own practice, let alone start a company from scratch."

Kyle furrowed his brow. "You're too hard on yourself, Laney. You have plenty of courage. You've moved to how many new places, all on your own?"

"It's not the same thing." She shook her head. "I'm talking about taking big risks, laying it all on the line. It's just not in me to do that."

A timer dinged in the kitchen, and Kyle stood up, but before he walked away he pinned her with a hard look. "It's not such a big risk when you know it's the real deal."

Was he still talking about the winery? Her stomach clenched, and she didn't know if she wanted him to be talking about her or not. *Not*. She pushed her hand flat against her abdomen and gave herself a mental shake.

"I've worked at the winery every summer since they bought the place, and never once did I doubt it would be a success." Kyle continued talking as he moved around the kitchen, pulling a covered casserole dish from the oven and setting out plates and cutlery. "At one point they couldn't make their mortgage payments, and helping them out was a dead easy decision."

So he was still talking about the winery. Laney turned around on the couch to better watch Kyle. He was mashing potatoes now, his light blue dress shirt rolled up to his elbows. She watched the muscles in his forearm flex and release as he worked butter and green onions into the mix in a stainless steel bowl. "You gave them a loan?"

"More like, I made a small investment in the company. I own two percent of the winery. So even if the wine wasn't any good, I'd still buy it." He winked at her, and her insides quivered again.

"You continue to surprise me."

"Mmmm? How else have I surprised you?" He tasted the potatoes, and reached for the pepper.

She pressed her lips together, not sure what to say. "You're still you, but...complicated isn't the right word. Busy, I guess. You're much busier than I would have thought. Helping neighbours, investing in a business, renovating your own place. The Kyle I knew would have wanted to spend his summers at the beach and his evenings watching TV or playing video games."

He put down the bowl of potatoes and leaned against the island. His face had that carefully neutral teacher facade in place. Her heart sank as she saw right past it. Some things about him hadn't changed, and a jaw twitch would make an appearance in three, two, one—

"That Kyle was twenty-two. He was an idiotic kid. I should hope that I'm a somewhat improved model. I'm a man. I don't shy away from hard work and I like to keep busy." He turned away from her and filled a small pot with water. "I have goals in life, Laney. I'm not sitting around."

She leapt to her feet, her heart in her throat. "I didn't mean... Kyle, you had goals back then. Big goals. I'm sorry. I've offended you."

He shook his head. "Now my goals are for myself."

She moved around the island, closing the gap between them, and wrapped her arms around his waist. Her face fit neatly between his shoulder blades. While it was an unusual way to assess vital signs, the doctor in her couldn't help but notice that while his respiration rate was normal, his heart rate was elevated. "I get it. I really do. I said something quite similar to my mom this morning, about me, I mean."

Kyle twisted to look at her and Laney eased her grip, allowing him to turn completely in her arms. His gaze was dark and searching, and she apologized again for ruining the mood. He shook his head and traced over her lips with his thumb.

"You didn't ruin anything. This isn't a date, not really. There's a lot of shit between us, Delaney, and we shouldn't pretend that there isn't. I don't need tonight to be light and breezy, I just need it to be real." He lowered his mouth to brush hers, soft and light at first, then hard and demanding, but with restraint. He dragged at her lower lip with his teeth, then smoothed over the swollen crest with the tip of his tongue before pulling back. "I have to put the beans on, can you refill our glasses?"

She nodded, too stunned to speak, and went to fetch the bottle from the living room.

Dinner was an unexpected delight. Braised thick pork chops in an orange and balsamic sauce with chunks of apples and onions, extra-buttery mashed potatoes and green beans on the side. Laney dug in, pausing every few bites to extol the awesomeness of his cooking and butter in general.

"I took a guess that you'd probably had enough quinoa and tofu over at the farm," Kyle chuckled as she swallowed more potatoes with a happy groan. "You haven't turned into a health food nut, have you?"

Laney shook her head. "I eat salad regularly and I try not to be a glutton, but I couldn't live like my sister does. I'm happy with my padding."

Kyle couldn't see any extra weight, but he knew better than to say anything. He'd seen Evie in her workout clothes, and he knew what Laney meant. They were both slim, but Laney had a softness to her curves while her sister's beauty was more about strength and definition—she looked like a professional dancer. Laney was more like the classic portrait of a ballerina, delicate and ethereal.

"Where did you learn to cook like that?" She set her fork and knife on her empty plate and turned toward Kyle. "That was amazing."

"Took lessons, watched the Food Network, practiced a lot." He shrugged. "It's no big deal."

"Uh, yes, it is. I live on takeout and leftovers brought in by my secretary. I wish I could cook like this. Where did you take lessons? I need to look into something like that."

"It was something through the city recreation catalogue." That Crystal had signed them up for. "I'm sure there would be a lot of options in Chicago."

Laney tilted her head to the side, as if she was trying to figure something out. "Ohhhhh. I get it. You took them with a girl." She nodded, like that made sense, which he didn't understand. Why wouldn't he take cooking classes on his own? "You've never liked the city rec programs. You always said they were—"

"—social, not educational. I can't believe you remember." That went back to his coaching days. He'd said the same thing to Crystal, but she just wanted to do something couple-y, she didn't care about how in-depth the course might be. "I was a bit harsh. It wasn't a bad class."

"I'll say, if it taught you how to cook like that. So, who did you go with? The ex?"

He shifted on his seat. "Yes, with Crystal."

"Awww, cute."

Kyle didn't like the edge to Laney's voice. He nudged her with his foot and nodded toward the sink. "Stick the plates over there, I'll get dessert out."

"You don't want to talk about her."

He raised an eyebrow. "You do?"

"Sure. We're friends, right? Friends can talk about anything."

He barked out a laugh. "Okay. Let's talk about your last boyfriend."

She pretended not to hear him as she started to rinse off the dinner plates. He stalked over and placed his hands against the counter on either side of her, trapping her next to the sink. He flicked off the tap and nudged his head against hers.

"I thought you wanted tonight to be honest." Laney's voice was quiet, but the hurt rang loud and clear.

"There's honest and then there's too much. Getting into twelve years of sexual history falls into the latter category. "

"I don't want to know about your sex life," she whispered. "I just...we didn't do anything like that. Couple stuff. I've never done that, with anyone. I'm curious."

"I'm not a great example of relationship success." That was an understatement. He didn't know how they'd ended up on this topic, and he couldn't see a way to navigate past it. Every muscle in his body was taut with tension, and he felt like a fight was just around the corner.

"Humour me." She pressed against him, making a pocket of space in which to turn, and then she was sliding her hands under his shirt. "Let's go sit by the fire and talk."

"I have a better idea. Let's go lie down by the fire, and I'll convince you that talking is overrated."

"That's been my line, hasn't it?" She laughed and twisted away from him, swaying her hips in the process. He groaned, wanting to grab those hips and slide her beneath him, kiss her until they both forgot how much was still left unsaid between them. He felt restless, like a boxer before a match, and he followed her, wondering if that feeling of discordance maybe couldn't be separated from the passion sparking between them. That this fling was actually makeup sex, or ex sex, delayed a decade.

Laney knelt on the rug and pulled off her top. He stood in front of her, taking in the glorious sight in front of him. Her blonde hair flowed loose down her back in gentle waves, cascading over the delicate curve of her shoulders. She wore a black pushup bra, her pale skin glowing in stark contrast despite the dim light in the room. She looked up at him with a gentle smile, but there was a faint tremble to her bottom lip. He stroked her cheek, and she rubbed her face back against his hand.

"Come down here," she whispered, tugging on his hand.

He pulled off his own shirt and joined her, pressing their bare torsos together, warming her on both sides as he dragged his hands up and down her spine. He dipped his head to capture her mouth and she pulled away. "Not yet. Let's talk."

Kyle groaned and ground his pelvis against her. "Feel that? He doesn't want to talk."

She grinned. "We have all night, remember?"

That earned her another groan, and he tucked his thumbs inside the waistband of her jeans. "Then why did we start to get naked?"

She tilted her head to the side and blinked as if just thinking about that question for the first time. "It seemed like a good idea. Like taking off armour. Plus I like it when you touch my breasts."

He stroked his thumbs around her hips, sending a shiver across her tummy, and then swept his hands north, mimicking the shape of her bra, his fingertips stroking the bare skin swelling over top of the cups. "Mmmm. I like that too."

"So you keep doing that, and let's talk."

"About what? It's a challenge to think when you're this close to me."

"I want to have healthy relationships."

"Do I look like Dr. Phil?" He slipped one bra strap off her shoulder, then the other. He left a trail of little kisses across her collarbone as he reached around behind her to do away with the undergarment completely. She gave a hitching little sigh when he sat back on his heels and pulled her up to straddle his lap. "Do you think I'm going to help you figure out how best to date other guys?" He thrust his hips hard against her and strummed across her nipples with his thumbs.

She swallowed hard. Two pink spots decorated her porcelain cheeks and her eyes dilated wide. "Why wouldn't you?" she gasped, arching her breasts toward his mouth.

He growled and flipped her over, his body pressing between her legs. He reached between them and undid the button of her jeans. "That's a good question," he said, sliding the zipper open. "Why don't you answer it while I make you come."

She gasped and pushed on Kyle's shoulders, wriggling out from underneath him. She held out a hand, as if to stop him from advancing again. "Wait," she panted. "Just ... stop for a second. This feels angry. Why does this feel angry?"

Kyle pushed himself to a stand and exhaled hard. "Fuck," he

hissed. "Dammit, I'm sorry, Laney. Here, come here." He pulled her up to join him. He grabbed a throw blanket from the chair and wrapped it around her. He stalked into the kitchen to grab another bottle of wine.

Laney shivered under the blanket. She didn't know why she couldn't just shut up. Kyle returned, with a bottle of wine in one hand and two glasses in the other. She gave him a small smile and was relieved when it was returned. He looked embarrassed, and she wanted to make it right.

"I'm not very good at this talking thing, clearly."

"We're both a bit out of practice." He poured two glasses, handed her one, then took a big gulp. "Two years, remember?"

"Try twelve." She grimaced.

"So you really haven't had a real relationship since we broke up?" He looked incredulous. "How did you fend them off?"

"I wasn't a nun." She took a sip of wine, then another. She glanced over at Kyle. He was beautiful, his long torso corded with muscles earned through manual labour, his abs tight and defined even as he leaned forward, elbows on his knees. She curved her hand around his bulging bicep and it flexed against her palm. "There haven't been that many guys."

He waved his hand. "I don't…I lost the right to care about that a long time ago."

She didn't argue. It was true, but it wasn't the only truth. "I don't like the idea of you being with anyone else either."

"Then why did you ask about Crystal? Why torture yourself?"

"Because I don't *want* to be jealous. I don't like that feeling. I don't like feelings in general."

Kyle turned toward her on the couch. The candle flickered, bouncing light off the side of his face and she sucked in a breath. His profile was beautiful, but full-on, his appeal was more base. He went from a statue to a hot blooded man, from fantasy to reality. Sexy, scary reality.

"I don't think that's true, Laney." The words slid between

them quietly, and he reached through them to caress her naked shoulder. "You like to feel me inside of you."

Her breath hitched. "That's different."

"Is it?" he murmured, tracing the line of her neck up to her jaw. He rubbed his fingers back and forth there, tipping her head to the side. He shifted closer and lowered his mouth to where her neck and shoulder meet.

She whimpered, the sound vibrating against his lips.

"Tell me this isn't a real feeling."

She couldn't. Her pulse sped up and he laid his palm flat on her chest. "In time, you'll want to feel here again."

Laney shook her head. She laced her fingers into Kyle's and pulled his hand lower to rest on her abdomen. "The agony here? I don't like to feel that. And it's inevitable, so this?" She pointed at her heart. "That's off limits. To everyone."

He didn't say anything until she went to move away. He pulled her closer instead and lowered his face so their foreheads pressed together. "That's my fault, then, and I'm sorry. To you, and all the men out there that probably want to love you. They're missing out."

She sniffed, and she realized that she was crying. *Fuck*. That wasn't how tonight was supposed to go down. He wiped her face with his hands and kissed her damp cheek. He meant it to comfort her, she knew that, but crying in front of him crossed a line. She felt way too vulnerable.

"I think I should go," Laney whispered, and Kyle nodded. She climbed off the couch, feeling clumsy as she searched for her shirt. She took her time putting it on and waited until she was composed before turning back to face him. "Well, it's been real."

He was across the room before she could crack a smile, and he hauled her into his arms. His hands gripped her shoulders, and uncomfortable heat radiated through her shirt. His gaze smouldered, and it took him a few moments to pull words together. "Don't make light of it, Laney. I get why you're leaving, but... fuck. You make me crazy."

Her gasp was cut off as he kissed her, bruising her lips. Probably her heart too. But Laney had tasted enough honesty for one night, so she buried that thought deep in the vault. His tongue pushed hard against hers, then softened, and she sank into the kiss. They were much better at this than they were at talking. Regret, longing and frustration flowed between them, and too quickly Kyle stepped away, and she stumbled at the loss. The scent of a date swirled around them, a mix of clean bodies, fancy drug store brands and fresh arousal, reminding her just how far off course the evening had gone. Without looking at her, he grabbed at his shirt and headed for the entryway. She followed, stuffing herself into winter gear. Kyle opened the door and she fled, not looking back.

13

Claire was reading in the living room when Laney got back. She closed her book but didn't get up. "How was dinner?"

Laney shrugged and made a little grimace. "About as well as one might expect dinner with an ex-boyfriend to go."

It wasn't a lie. And it was all she was going to share. She waved her mother back to her book and headed upstairs. Evie had fallen asleep in the boys' room during story time, and Laney pulled the door closed, not wanting to wake any of them up. She needed a long, hot soak in the tub.

The bubbly heat warmed her from the inside out, but it didn't do anything to shake the discontent. She dunked under the water and shook her head, her hair floating around her like bands of ribbon. Where had the evening gone wrong? The more she thought about fighting with Kyle, and leaving him without resolving the tension that had been brewing between them, the worse she felt. She hated that uneasy niggle at the back of her neck, but she didn't know how to make it go away.

She had to admit that tonight revealed they still had a lot of unresolved issues, and it was probably impossible to have a no-strings attached fling with her ex. Her stomach flipped at the idea that whatever was going on between them was now over.

No.

Laney sat straight up in the bath with a gasp, her instant, visceral rejection shocking even as she felt the truth of it.

She wanted more.

But with Kyle?

He wasn't easily duplicated. Twelve years had proven that point. She swiped at her face, pushing water away from her eyes and that errant desire from her mind, but both dripped back undeterred. Was she falling for Kyle after all? Considering that question was like tiptoeing to the edge of a cliff, and she inhaled a shaky breath.

Memories both old and new rolled over in her head.

The first time Kyle kissed her. She grinned. She had actually kissed him. He'd come to the university library to help her study, and found her in the stacks trying to get a book on the top shelf. A friendly hug turned into a full body press, then she'd pulled his face to hers. She could still feel the pounding of his heart against hers, how his palms went damp in the small of her back, and the unbearable ache in her heart when he pulled away.

That didn't hold a candle to the misery of walking away from him for good when she left for Harvard. And nothing she'd experienced since coming home compared to any of the low points of their relationship. Relief rolled through her body.

She dressed in flannel pyjama pants, a t-shirt and thick wool work socks. Looking at her bed, she decided she needed a fortifying cup of hot chocolate first and padded downstairs. Her mother had moved to the kitchen and was turning out the lights.

"Can I get you something, sweetie?"

"I just came down to make some hot chocolate. Do you want some?"

Claire shook her head and yawned, so Laney shooed her toward the stairs. "I'll be up in a few minutes."

Claire paused and touched Laney's cheek. "You okay?"

She nodded. She would be, anyway.

She got the kettle on the stove, then dug out the powdered hot chocolate mix. There was even a bag of marshmallows in the back of the cupboard.

Something scratched at the door as she reached for the whistling kettle. She jumped and whirled around. *Someone.*

With a finger to her lips, Laney pulled the door open. "What are you doing here?" she whispered.

Kyle stepped in, careful not to make any noise with his boots. "I won't stay long," he said, matching her quiet tone. "But I just couldn't let you go to bed on that note."

It was dangerous, how much she liked him saying that. She reached for his gloved hand, the leather cold against her flushed fingers, still warm from the bath. Pulling him inside her mother's kitchen was dangerous too—and not because they needed to sneak around.

She wanted to press up on her toes and lace her arms around his neck. She settled for staying close while he unzipped his coat, then she took it from him.

If she took a surreptitious sniff of it as she hung it on a chair, that was her guilty little secret.

"Are you making hot chocolate?" He asked after pulling her in for a hug. She looked up at him, then followed his gaze to where he was eyeing the canister on the counter.

"Maybe." She grinned as he tightened his hold on her.

"Can I have some?"

She sniffed, mock-considering saying no. "Don't you have any at home?"

"I do, but it's a cold walk back." He gestured at the driveway.

He hadn't driven his truck over. He shrugged, as if there wasn't an easy explanation.

That was the truth for so much of what was going on between them, what was a late night walk in the cold? Maybe he needed the walk to clear his head, or maybe he didn't want to alert her mother and the neighbours about the late night visit—although Laney had just driven over to his place and back again.

But it didn't matter. Complicated or not, she was glad to see him again, so she pointed to the table. And just because it helped the narrative in her head to pretend this was like the good ol' days, she put her finger to her lips again.

Smiling as he gave her an exaggerated nod, she pulled down another mug, then stirred sweetened cocoa powder into hot water and topped both cups with a splash of cream and two floating marshmallows.

A quick rummage through the cupboards didn't turn up anything other than spelt cookies, so she carried just the cups to the table.

"I'm sorry, I don't have anything sweet to offer." As she said that, she realized that she'd left Kyle's place before they'd gotten to dessert, and her hand flew to her mouth as she gasped. "Your dessert!"

He shook his head and wrapped his hands around his cup. "Don't worry about it. It wasn't homemade, or anything. This is great."

Laney slumped in her chair. She felt rotten.

"Hey, don't make that face. It's fine, really. I don't have enough drama in my life." Kyle winked at her. "And I only had a few days to soak up whatever you can throw at me. Since you aren't actually throwing anything, it's all good."

She wasn't convinced, but she didn't want to get into anything again so she nodded and smiled. "Will it keep? The dessert, I mean. Maybe we could try again tomorrow night. I don't need to be back in Chicago until New Year's."

Kyle shook his head, clear disappointment on his face. "I'm curling tomorrow with a bunch of teachers. I probably won't be home until late."

"Call me when you're done and I'll come over."

"Are you looking for a booty call?" He raised an eyebrow and pulled out his phone.

"I think we've demonstrated that works better for us than the whole 'dinner and a movie' thing, don't you?" Laney regretted the words as soon as they were out of her mouth. Dinner had been great. Kyle didn't look offended, though, and she took his phone and added her number, and then after a moment's hesitation, her email address and Twitter handle as well.

"Twitter?" Kyle asked, looking at her profile.

She shrugged. "It's a good way to stay connected with other physicians and keep up to date on news in the medical community. I've done a bit of guest blogging too. I just added it because your address book has a field for it. You don't need to follow me."

Kyle met her gaze for a beat, then finished his hot chocolate and rinsed the mug in the sink. Laney stood to see him out to the door, and after he pulled on his coat, he took one of her hands in his while he held his gloves in the other. He rubbed his thumb over her knuckles, back and forth, and she squeezed his fingers. "I'm going to follow you, Laney."

———

KYLE DIDN'T USE Twitter nearly as often as Laney, but he had an account that he used to share education links and weigh in— diplomatically—on relevant discussions.

What he never did was wake up and reach for his phone to check the latest tweets.

But after he'd stayed up late scrolling through her feed, and then reading her blog, that was exactly what he did.

Waking up and thinking about Laney was dangerous. Giving in to that hunger just twisted her deeper under his skin. It was a good thing that he'd stuck to his plans to go curling. It was a full day event, and he could have ducked out of it—almost guaranteed, when he got there, someone would ask why he'd showed up instead of spending the day with Laney.

There were no secrets in Wardham. There was a healthy amount of speculation, which often sent people spiralling toward incorrect assumptions.

Except in this case, maybe it wasn't that incorrect.

He was hung up on her. He always would be. He scrubbed his

hand over his face as he kicked off the blanket and told himself to get out of bed.

Then he rolled onto his side and opened the Twitter app instead. No new tweets, so he click on her profile and followed the link to her faculty website at the university. Assistant Professor of Medicine. Board-certified surgeon. Smelled like strawberries and laughed during sex, then wrapped herself around him again.

He was more than hung up on her. And she was leaving in a few days.

He needed to go curling. Have a few beers and shoot the shit with his co-workers.

Maybe after he jerked off in the shower.

———

THE ANNUAL WARDHAM Elementary Bonspiel ended, as it usually did, with catcalls, smack talk, and accusations of cheating.

Then everyone headed to Danny's, Wardham's only pub, for a few rounds of beer.

Kyle had enjoyed a few over the day, but as they settled at a long table in the back, he ordered Coke instead.

"Are you the designated driver?" the bartender asked. Mari always made him feel old, because she was best friends with his little cousin, Stella, who was an adult now, but he still thought of them both as teenagers.

"Not unless they are planning to head home in thirty minutes. I'm just here for one round tonight."

She gave him a knowing wink. Jesus Christ. Now the gossip had reached beyond his immediate social circle. Fantastic. And teenagers—who were actually adults—were giggling about his dating life again.

"You're heading out?" Jim, the grade seven teacher, asked.

Kyle thought about giving the same excuse he'd just given

Mari. But he didn't need to hide his evening plans. "Have an old girlfriend to catch up with. She's just in town for a few days."

"Nice." Jim didn't know the Calhouns. He didn't even live in Wardham, but the next town over.

"Yeah, it has been."

"Where is she now?"

"Chicago."

"Nice. Went there for a weekend with my wife last summer. Saw a ball game."

"Fun." He was definitely broaching the idea of a visit to Laney. He'd never been. At the very least, it would be a good chance to see the city. "What else did you do there?"

"Waterfront cruise. You gotta go see that bean statue thing. And the pizza...actually, all the food. There's this Polish restaurant that makes the world's best pirogies. My God. You thinking of visiting?"

"Yeah, maybe."

"Life is short."

Yeah, he was finally learning that lesson.

14

"Squeeze your butt! Maintain a straight line through your ribs and tummy, good, now slow inhale, and exhale, hold it there, good, inhale again, slow, that's good." Evie had missed her calling as a drill sergeant, although after a week of these exercises, Laney had to admit that her core did feel stronger. Not that she'd actually confess that out loud.

"And with this exhale, you'll come out of shoulder bridge, maintaining a neutral spine. Roll down to the mat, then up to a seated position. Connor will lead the next exercise."

Laney grinned at her nephew. "Whatcha got for us, big guy?"

Connor put his hands on his hips. "This is an advanced move, it's really for superheroes, but you can try it. It's called superman flying supertwist. Max is going to demonstrate."

Max came running in wearing a tea towel as a cape, which he whipped off and flung at Laney's head. He threw himself onto her mat, flat on his stomach, arms and legs stretched out and lifted slightly off the ground.

"Super Max, roll over. Uh, on the, you know, exhale." Without touching the ground with either his hands or feet, Max flipped effortlessly to his back, then returned with similar ease to his front. "Once you've mastered that move—" Laney and Claire exchanged skeptical looks "—then you can add the twist. Super Max, fly!"

Max started to rock from side to side, wriggling his body, and Laney skittered backward off the mat to give him more room. He flipped once, and then again, and finished with a triumphant 90 degree turn, settling into a flying Superman pose, with the unique Max flair of using his hands as pretend laser guns. The three women dissolved into giggles, and Evie led them through a few final stretches.

"Maybe you and Connor should run family Pilates classes," Laney suggested as they wandered to the kitchen for some home-made protein bars.

Evie nodded. "Honestly, I've been thinking about it. I'll need to find a different space, because the studio space I'm sharing right now is fully booked. I'm only doing six classes a week, all adult, and they're too popular to change."

"If you got a dedicated space, how many classes could you offer?" Laney was surprised to hear that her sister wanted to expand. Evie seemed quite happy with her part-time schedule.

Evie shrugged. "Me personally? I could do four a day, although I'd rather hire part-time instructors and just lead one or two myself. I've drafted up a schedule with classes every day of the week, but in order to make a go of a standalone studio, I think I'd need to partner with a complimentary service. Maybe a spa. It's still in the early planning stages."

Laney gaped at her sister. "I had no idea. That all sounds fantastic. If you need anything...what's mine is yours, you know that, right?"

Evie nodded. "Thank you. It won't be necessary, but I appreciate it. If I can change the subject..."

"No, you can't." Laney shook her head, and stuffed a protein bar into Evie's mouth. "I'm going to shower, then I think we should watch *Love Actually*."

The diversion worked, and while Evie opened her mouth to ask again a few times during the movie, she thought better of it each time. The afternoon flew by, and after dinner, Laney reflected on how nice the day had been without any discussion. *Talking is overrated*, she decided, and that gave her an idea.

Kyle sent her a text shortly after nine o'clock saying he was heading home. She smoothed a hand across her outfit, borrowed from Evie—a denim miniskirt and a black long sleeve stretch shirt that looked conservative at first blush, but up close was thin enough to reveal the shadow of her black bra and the long delicate silver necklace she wore nestled between her breasts. She finished the outfit with her thigh high grey knit stockings and Evie's hooker boots. She left her hair down, and didn't bother with much makeup—only smudge proof mascara and peach flavoured lip balm.

She tucked the piece of paper she needed into the micro pocket on the skirt and squeezed her thighs together in anticipation.

She stopped in the living room to say goodnight to Evie and Claire. Her mother raised an eyebrow at her outfit, and Evie gave her an enthusiastic thumbs up, so she knew she'd hit the right tone. Tonight was a hook-up, plain and simple. Nothing else would work between them. Not just because of geography. There was too much history. Too much mess and not enough time. She squeezed her eyes shut. *If only*…but there was no point finishing that thought. And why bother? The sex, when they didn't stuff it up with chit-chat, was knee-wobblingly good. A faint tremor started low in her belly. Kyle inside her. His mouth on her. Hungry kisses and big warm hands touching all over, making her melt. She was going to be soaking wet before she made it down the road at the rate her mind was going.

––––––––

KYLE STOOD in the middle of his house. After having a quick shower and putting clean sheets on the bed, he wasn't sure what to do next. Candles and wine had been too much the night before. Laney had asked about dessert. Should he unlock the door and just wait for her in bed? And why the hell was he so nervous? He decided to pull the cheesecake out of the fridge and leave it on the island along with a bowl of grapes and bottles of wine, Canadian Club, and sparkling water. Cover all the bases.

Laney's headlights flared through the window.

At the door, she silenced his greeting with a light, breathless kiss and stepped past him. She wore an impossibly short skirt and sexy as hell boots, and once he took her coat, he could see the outline of her bra and something shiny through her shirt. She was breathtaking. He opened his mouth to tell her just how gorgeous she was when she stepped close and pressed her finger against his lips. She handed him a folded up piece of paper.

Talking is overrated. Let's see how we do communicating with our bodies instead.

He raised an eyebrow, and she returned the expression with impish challenge. One he would accept, no question. She was all long legs, feisty heat and naughty promises. He couldn't resist.

He extended his hand and she laced her fingers into his, letting him lead her into the living room. The silence was weird, but he'd do anything to keep that secret smile on Laney's face. He pulled his phone out of his pocket and thumbed through his playlists quickly, looking for something country. She used to love Faith Hill, which he didn't have, but hopefully the albums he'd downloaded over the holidays would be an acceptable soundtrack for the night. He set his phone on the speaker docking station on the side table and tugged Laney into his arms as the first strum of guitar filled the room. She trembled, and he closed his eyes for a moment, willing himself not to want more than what was right in front of him. *Everything I've ever wanted.*

Everything he let slip away, too long ago.

And it wasn't that he'd fumbled. Fights happened. Mistakes happened.

It was that he hadn't even tried to catch her as she pulled away. He didn't go to her when he had all the chances in the world. Didn't read her emails, not that there'd been that many.

Like more would have made a difference?

And here she was, tonight, by some small miracle, and he wasn't happy with that. Never enough.

Mother fu—the realization hit him like a Mack truck, and he tensed his hands on her gently rocking hips.

Laney looked up at him, her eyes soft with appreciation. She crinkled her brow, questioning whatever she saw on his face, and he shut the door on his dwelling.

She was enough.

A week with Laney had filled him with happiness in a way that work, his house, even his friends and family didn't. In a way his two years alone certainly hadn't. He hadn't been unhappy, not by a long shot, but this was...transcendent.

He didn't know what the future would hold, but tonight, he'd hold Laney, and it would be enough.

Her lips curved, pleased with the changing look in his eyes, maybe, and she tucked her head against his shoulder. The air was still thick with all that they couldn't talk about.

Fear.

History.

Distance.

But as she wrapped her arms around his neck and they swayed together, their earnest desire for each other won out and he let his hands roam down her supple body.

His palms cupped her bottom, and she lifted her hips in response, pressing his erection into her belly, and he had to wrap one arm around her waist to keep them both upright as her back arched. He kissed her lips, then her jaw, neck and collarbone, and as his mouth travelled south, so too did his other hand, curling under the hem of her skirt. He was rewarded with delicious bare skin at the top of her thigh, and he made a mental note to tell her just how hot those stockings were once they were allowed to speak. He stroked around to her hip, then held his palm there against the edge of her underwear. She got to set the ground rules, he would set the pace.

He had three goals. Get lost in Laney, make it last all night, and not think about the fact that they were on borrowed time to get this right. Her leaving Wardham thinking that she was better off without him, again, ripped a jagged tear through his guts. That she was leaving was crystal clear, but he wanted it to be on good terms. Friendly terms. Maybe ones with benefits.

The music changed to a slower ballad. He slid both hands to cup her face and brushed her lips with his, more a promise than a full out kiss. She swayed against him, and he realized she was dancing. He smiled, and she must have felt it against her mouth, because she opened her eyes and leaned her head back a bit. Her gaze roamed over his face, and whatever she saw, she liked, because she gave him a dazzling smile. Yeah, he could dance for a bit.

He shifted their bodies so he could move them as one. His hands on her hips, his knee between her legs. He thought about the exposed tops of her thighs spreading open and his erection pulsed, like he needed any reminding about where his cock wanted to be. But he wanted to savour the anticipation. Smell her hair and wonder what the shiny thing was under her top. Let her shimmy against him until she broke her own rule and begged him to move to the bed.

A wet tongue at the base of his neck tested that resolve. Maybe their shirts could go. He tugged at Laney's top first, giving her the silent instruction. While she pulled it over her head, he threw off his own henley and then reached for her hands, tugging them to his own waist before he palmed her hips again. He clenched his abs under her cool touch, and she responded with even lighter circles, tickling him until he lost whatever small bit of rhythm he'd pretended to have. He hoisted her up in his arms and tossed her onto the couch with a growl and she giggled. That lilting laugh undid him every time, and he fell to his knees beside the couch, curving over her pale, soft body to scatter kisses on her stomach.

Her boots were next to capture his attention, and he easily

lifted one leg, then the other, unzipping and tossing the footwear into a dark corner of the room. Her skirt hitched up, well above the tops of her stockings, and in the shadow of his body, black boy shorts were the only scrap of fabric left between him and nirvana. He grazed her skin with his palm, fingers settling comfortably into the space between the tops of her thighs. She arched into his touch, and he watched her face soften as she gave herself over to longing. They didn't need words for him to know what she was asking.

Their breathing slowed at the same time. She needed him just as much as he needed her. Her gaze locked onto his, and he exhaled again, louder this time. She squirmed under his fingers as he traced over her fabric covered centre.

She mewled, and with his other hand he pressed a finger to her lips. She smiled under his touch, and he couldn't hold himself back. He climbed on top of her, his left hand between them, still teasing her core, and scorched her mouth with his. This was a kiss loaded with meaning.

Need.

Desire.

Promise.

Laney pressed her hands against the hard planes of his chest, then trailed lower. He held himself above her, braced on his forearm, and he started to shake as her fingers tickled the subtle ridges of his abdomen. She bit her lip and eased her palm against the flat of his belly behind his waistband. Her eyes widened as she realized he was commando, and he returned the raised eyebrow look. *Touch me*, he silently begged, but she pulled back to undo his jeans. Her knuckles rubbed against skin as she worked the button, and he jerked his hips toward her. The rasp of his zipper was sweet relief, and he couldn't hold back a groan as she wrapped her hand around his shaft.

He needed to touch bare skin.

Damn it, he needed to taste bare skin.

He rocked back and forth in her hand first, his palm resting flat on her sex, then pulled away. He sucked in a ragged breath. First step, get her to the bed.

————

Kyle loomed large above her, bare chested, jeans unbuttoned and obscenely low on his hips. He looked lean and hard.

Very hard.

She sucked in a breath of her own and wriggled out of her skirt. He slid his arms around her and hoisted her over his shoulder as she yelped in surprise. He slapped her ass for making noise. She would have protested if that wasn't against the rules. Her rules. And if being spanked didn't make her slippery with want. She blushed at the realization.

He crossed to the bed in a few long strides, and before he let her down, he stripped off her socks and underwear. Only then did he relax his grip around her waist, and she slid down his body. But he stopped her before she got to the good stuff. Instead, he held her hard against his chest, and his fingers got busy. One hand flicked her bra open, the other palmed her bare ass, teasing her slick wet heat with the lightest of strokes from behind. Her hips flexed, seeking firmer contact. He shuddered against her, and eased her back on the soft mattress. He shucked his jeans, then followed her down. She ached from wanting him, and his descent took far too long. Panting hard, she grasped his erection and lifted her hips to drive him home, but he shifted as well, evading what they both wanted.

He shuddered again, and then she saw it. His control was shredded, and he didn't want this to end. What had he asked for? More than a stolen moment.

He wanted this to last all night. They didn't need to rush.

She stretched out, laying herself bare beneath him.

This was so different than what they'd once had. She'd thought their summer together had been perfection. Discovering sex with Kyle had been magical, but she'd been naive. It hadn't been perfect. At the first sign of stress, their fledgling relationship had crumbled. Coming together after all this time, finding passion again in the long buried ashes...different barely scratched the surface in describing it.

As Kyle mouthed his way down her body, as he lifted her thighs to his shoulders and held her hips right where he wanted them, Laney realized this was more than they'd ever had. It wasn't perfect. It was complicated and messy, but as his tongue stroked her, lifting her high and tossing her into a wave of pleasure, it hit her.

This is real.

Time stood still as he loved her with his mouth, then his hands, and finally his whole body, hip to hip, chest to chest, mouth to mouth. He held her gaze as he thrust into her again and again, sure and steady, as if to say, *this could be our every night. This should be our forever.* Matching tremors wracked through their bodies, as if his orgasm triggered hers and vice versa. As if they were one.

He pinned her against him as he rolled to his side. She almost cried out at the loss of his weight. She didn't know what time it was, but it was certainly late.

He stroked her back, his fingers running leisurely up and down her spine. They were both covered in sweat, and tingling trails lingered in the wake of his movement. Perspiration had never felt so wicked before. She shivered, and he indicated they should get up. He led her into the shower, where they quietly washed each other. It wasn't that the heat between them had gone, exactly, but this wasn't the overt sexuality of earlier. This was caring. Connection.

Under the hot stream of water, they held each other, foaming bubbles sluicing off their bodies. Laney almost broke the silence a few times, but what was there to say?

15

———————

The warm, heavy body draped around her was Laney's first clue that she'd fallen asleep in Kyle's bed. She blinked. It was still the middle of the night because she couldn't see anything, although that could also be because her face was buried in Kyle's shoulder. His left arm and leg were thrown over her body, his hands twisted in her hair. A bead of sweat rolled between her breasts. She tried to roll to her back, but her bedmate had her pinned between impressively defined biceps, even at rest, and his forearms looped behind her shoulders. She nudged him and he tugged her closer, his lips brushing her forehead.

"Don't go."

"I won't. I just need—" *some space* "—to go to the bathroom."

He grunted and released her, his fingers trailing over her body as she slipped out of bed. She stood at the curtain, watching as he flopped over onto his stomach. His arms spanned the width of the bed, his feet hung off the end. He took her breath away, even in his sleep. It wasn't just that he was rugged and handsome. He also oozed pheromones. She shook her head. No, it wasn't simple chemistry. They were good together. *Great. Best ever, by a mile.* But not just because of attraction. The spark got them naked, but then the things they did together, the choices they freely made with one another, all of that was extraordinary. A level of intimacy that she'd shied away from for far too long, that she'd let become so foreign it should make her blush. She touched her cheek, acknowledging that standing in the dark, watching her lover sleep, she probably *was* blushing a bit.

But she didn't feel any reluctance or embarrassment, didn't regret anything that they did. Because everything they did together felt right, and oh so good. With previous lovers, it was all about finding what worked and what didn't, and she often established boundaries. Laney couldn't think of anything that she wouldn't want to do with Kyle. She waited for her face to flush at the naughty thoughts that were racing through her mind, but the only physical response was a tremor in her belly. She couldn't give him forever, but she could give him an unforgettable *right now*.

She padded first to the washroom, then to the kitchen. They never did get to dessert, and her stomach rumbled as she saw the white bakery box spotlighted on the island when she flicked on the lights. Her eyes flicked to the bedroom. Would he mind? She could see his raised eyebrow in her mind's eye and laughed quietly. She deserved a midnight snack.

She peeked inside and let out a quiet gasp at the glistening blueberry cheesecake. A delicate perfume of fruitiness made her mouth water, and she quickly sourced a plate, fork and serving knife. The fruit sat plump and shiny, scattered at random across a thin red-purple glaze poured over the top of the creamy white cake. Laney didn't want to mar the perfection, but she was dying to know what that fresh scent tasted like in her mouth.

"Can I join you?" She whirled around, the server gripped in her hand, and Kyle flashed a sleepy grin at her jumpiness. "Sorry to startle you. I got cold and lonely."

The unintended pout in his last words tugged at her gut. He didn't seem to notice as he wrapped a warm arm around her waist and nuzzled his face into her neck. Then he took over, lifting a large wedge of cake onto the plate and gestured for her to follow him to the bed area, now bathed in the soft glow of his reading lamp. They climbed onto the mattress and sat facing each other, cross-legged, with the blanket covering their laps, the plate resting on Kyle's knee between them. He offered her the first bite, and she closed her eyes as the tangy flavours rioted across her tongue. It was smooth and sweet, with a hint of citrus. Lemon? No, lime. Heavy enough to be decadent, but it melted in her mouth and she groaned for more.

"Where on earth did you get this?" She plucked the last bit of ginger biscuit crust off the plate with nimble fingers. As Kyle pouted, she waved her hand to the kitchen. "Oh no! You want more, it's out there. This bite is all mine."

"It's amazing, eh? Carrie offers a limited number of take-home desserts every day. She's a goddess." Laney arched her eyebrow, and Kyle let out a gentle laugh. "She's also my sister-in-law. She owns the bakery in town. Bun in the Oven?"

She let out a sigh of relief and the laughter grew. *Dammit.* "The redhead. Karen's best friend." He nodded, lips still twitching in mirth. "Right. I met her when I was in town on Christmas Eve, she seems lovely."

Kyle set the plate aside and tugged her toward him for a soft kiss. "You're lovely."

"I can't bake like this. Or at all."

"You don't need to, that's why we have Carrie in our lives."

He meant his family, but the inadvertent reference to the two of them as a single unit still did something funny in her chest. "It's a bit far for me to drive just for cheesecake."

"There's more for you here than just dessert." This time the suggestion was clear and deliberate, and that funny feeling crystalized into bittersweet pain. Kyle flicked off the light and tugged her into the crook of his arm. "I don't want to freak you out, or push you, at all. I like you, a lot, and I don't see why this—" he waved his hand over their bodies "—needs to be a one-time thing."

Laney swallowed hard around the lump in her throat, and she

willed herself not to cry. If she cried, she would run away, and much to her surprise, she didn't want to do that this time. She wanted to tough out this conversation and get to the other side. "Oh, Kyle," she said with a heavy breath. "I don't see how it can be anything but. My life is in Chicago, and that's not going to change."

"You don't see yourself ever moving back home?" Kyle asked the big question without judgment or expectation, and a tiny fissure split the surface of her heart. Every step of her career had taken her further from Wardham, from Kyle, and now she was realizing too late that she didn't leave an emergency hatch in the master plan. Even if they explored a long-distance relationship, her life had no room for compromise. No room for her to be the true partner that Kyle deserved. She couldn't lead him on. She took a deep breath, and swallowed past the growing knot.

"It would be impossible." She shook her head. "I can practice plastic surgery a bit closer, but more cosmetic stuff. I work with a cleft palate reconstruction team at the children's hospital..."

"And there's nothing like that here." To her surprise, Kyle nodded. "You feel really strongly about making a difference for those children."

"How did you..." Laney pulled her head up and stared at Kyle.

He shrugged. "Twitter."

She sank into his chest. His heartbeat was slow and steady. Why was he not more shaken by the conversation? Another fissure slithered into existence and she blinked hard. His hand stroked up and down her back, calm and sure, and nothing made sense. "Kyle..."

"Shhh. It's okay."

It wasn't, and she didn't know how to fix it. "I wish we had more time."

"I'll come and visit you. March Break maybe, or the summer."

Yes, please. She selfishly wanted to block off all long weekends and holidays in both of their calendars. Shame flooded her gut at the half-life she could offer him. "Is that a good idea?"

"Is it a bad idea?"

"There's no happy ending for us." Her voice cracked. "Probably easier to deal with that now and figure out a way to stay friends."

Kyle didn't say anything, but he kept stroking her back as if she hadn't just tried to break up with him. The silence stretched, and she realized he wasn't going to respond.

"Kyle?"

"Laney?" She swore she could hear a smile in his voice, and she twisted around to see his face. He gazed back at her with a curious look. "Do we need to have this conversation right now?"

She didn't know when would ever be a good time. *Never. Stop trying to break up with him. Move back to Wardham and have all of his babies.* This time the fissure wasn't so small, and as her heart split in two, she felt the first tear slip down the side of her nose.

"No, no, no. Damn it, why are you crying?" Kyle rolled her underneath him, holding himself up above her body with his forearms. He nuzzled her nose with his, grabbing her gaze.

"I can't give you what you want."

"I want you."

"You want your own family photo to add to the collection on the fridge." She sniffed, her breath hitching in her chest. "You want kids and a life here. Family dinners and the like."

———

HE THOUGHT he was prepared for any objection, but he hadn't planned on that one. "You don't want a family?"

Fat tears rolled down her cheeks as she shook her head in misery. "It's not about want. It's just not feasible with my life. Not like what you want."

A lot of different words crowded to the tip of his tongue, but none sounded just right. This was too important to guess at, so

Kyle just tipped his head, touching his forehead to Laney's. He hoped she could see how much he loved her in his eyes. He wanted to tell her, but not in response to tears or drama.

Her breath was still hitching in her chest as she tried to stifle little sobs, and he smoothed over her hair and down her cheek. "Shhhh. Sweetheart, it's okay."

"Stop say..saying that." She turned her head to the side, pressing her face into the pillow.

Kyle rolled off her with a sigh. Nothing she could say would sway how he felt, or what he was going to do, but he didn't want to steamroll her either. He traced lazy patterns on her back until her breathing returned to normal, trying to show her in actions what she didn't want to hear.

He wouldn't trade Laney for an alternate life with children and another woman as his wife. There was no doubt in his mind about that. If she didn't want children, then they wouldn't have any. But she was wrong about not wanting a family. Kyle was going to be there, steady and quiet and constant, until she realized that they were a unit.

It wasn't going to happen overnight. He wouldn't walk away from his job, so he had told her the truth. The next step was him visiting Chicago on the next school break. And maybe setting up some appointments with elementary school principals while he was there. He turned the plan over in his mind, pleased with himself. He opened his mouth to tell Laney in no uncertain terms that she was everything he could ever want, but the words died in his throat when her phone rang.

She leapt out of bed with a curse. Who would be calling her in the middle of the night? Kyle followed her into the main room. She glanced at the display and swore again. Kyle's heart sank as she answered.

"Rick? What are you...Oh. My god, are you okay?...No, I'm still in Wardham. I told you I probably wouldn't be home until the 30th..." She threw an apologetic look in Kyle's direction and wandered into the kitchen.

He didn't bother to follow. He didn't want to hear half of her conversation with some guy named Rick, who was familiar enough to call her in the middle of the night when he had a problem. He didn't want to draw any unfair conclusions about this asshole who got hear her say the word "home" and mean the city that they both lived in. They hadn't talked explicitly about being exclusive, though, and Kyle sank to the couch. He shook his head. He wasn't going there. *Liar, you've already gone there.*

"...I'm almost six hours away, and I haven't slept much tonight...That's none of your business. I can take your shift the next night, though. I'll head back later today."

Laney ended the call and came over to join Kyle on the couch. She laid her hand on his arm. "I have to..."

"I know, I heard." He couldn't keep the hurt out of his voice. He hated that he had been so confident five minutes earlier, and one work-related call tore that to shreds. How could he promise that he could fit into her life when it would be months of this before they lived in the same place? Deja vu swept over him and he realized that he'd been at this same crossroads before.

It was the day before Laney was to leave for Harvard. She had slept over at his place the night before, but that night she was going back to the farm. The thought of not seeing her again until Thanksgiving tore him up inside. She had been telling him about her future classmates who she'd connected with already online. He had never experienced raw jealousy before, and it tore through him like bright green toxic waste.

"Just don't go and fall in love with any of those Harvard douchebags, okay?"

"Kyle, don't... Please be excited for me."

"It's hard to be excited about only seeing you a handful of times over the next year."

"We'll talk every night."

"Until you get too busy with studying."

Each barb was a spark on dry tinder, and neither noticed until it was too late. The fight was long and drawn-out. There were many points where Kyle could have pulled back, could have apologized and saved the relationship, but he was too angry to think straight. He couldn't remember most of what he said, but he'd never forget the last poison tipped dart he whipped at her before she walked out.

"Med school can't keep you warm at night. It won't rub your feet or give you babies. I love you Laney, too bad that's not enough for you."

He hadn't thought about those words in a long time. Regret lanced through him. He had damaged more than their relationship that day.

Now it was the middle of the night and she was needed at a hospital five hundred kilometres away. Kyle pulled Laney hard against his chest. "Go do what you have to do. Call me when you get a chance. I'll come and visit. I've got Red Bull, remember? Gotta make a road trip somewhere, might as well be Chicago."

"I'm sorry," She mumbled into his neck. "I thought we'd have another day."

He tugged her high enough to steal a kiss. "Don't worry about it."

"I didn't want to say goodbye like this."

"We're not."

Pain twisted across her face. He wanted to ease that for her, but he knew she wouldn't believe him. Not yet.

"I'm not asking you for anything." Kyle cupped her face in his hands. "I'm just saying that I'll see you again soon. That's on me to make happen, and I will. Promise."

Laney nodded and brushed her lips against his one last time. He helped her up and watched her get dressed. When she pulled on her coat, he took the zipper slider out of her hand and fit it to the opposite pin. The quiet rasp of metal teeth fitting together filled the silence. There was too much to say in not enough time.

16

———

The empty call room wasn't the Hilton, or her condo, but it would suffice for a nap. Laney could go home and leave the senior resident in charge until she was needed next, but chances were high that she'd be paged before her ass hit the couch at home. They had been called for consults in both the pediatric and adult emergency departments almost non-stop, and Laney had just come out of a four hour operation on a thirteen year old who just barely survived a motor vehicle accident. There was a reason she worked on the pediatric reconstruction team and at Derma-North instead of providing regular on-service support. As a resident she had loved the rush of these shifts, but now she longed for a regular schedule with patients scheduled at least a day in advance. She liked the routine of clinic days and out-patient care.

She tucked her arm under her head as a makeshift pillow. If only it was Kyle's bicep. His body could be her blanket. His inevitable erection her alarm clock. Laney groaned and rolled over. She'd arrived in Chicago yesterday at noon and sent a quick text to both Kyle and Evie telling them that she was safe and sound. Then she stopped at the store to pick up bananas and yogurt, had a nap, gone for a run, written a blog post and was in bed fast asleep by eight.

Twenty-four hours later, she still hadn't called him. He'd sent two texts, both short and sweet. She should respond in kind, but she couldn't summon the inner flirt right now. She was stuck in a sad melancholy. If she called, she'd probably cry. She'd tell him how much she missed him, that March was too far away. She'd promise the moon just to see him again. Maybe he could fly from Detroit, or they could meet halfway and spend the weekend in a seedy motel.

And then real life would inevitably crash down upon them. He'd want her to come for one of his many family events, and she'd have on-service call, or a conference, or a patient flown in from overseas. He deserved to be someone's number one priority. And then sooner than later, the conversation would turn to kids and choosing a home, and there was only heartbreak to be found there. They had fixed themselves on perpendicular trajectories a long time ago, and by some freak violation of the laws of trigonometry, they'd had a second momentary intersection. But time doesn't stand still, and their lives would drag them apart. Again.

Laney's pager went off and she sat up. *Doesn't that just prove the point? Can't even fantasize about my boyfriend without interruption.*

She was halfway down the hall to the ER before the label sank in. She shoved the freak-out deep down inside, and redirected the burst of adrenaline toward dealing with whatever was on the other side of the curtain.

The sun was up by the end of her shift, but downtown Chicago was still bathed in cool grey shadows. Traffic was limited, and she savoured the quiet. She covered the few blocks to her condo at a slower pace than usual. The frigid air nipped at her cheeks, and she tugged her hat lower to cover her ears. Her phone vibrated in her pocket and she smiled when she pulled it out.

"How was your shift?" Kyle's voice washed over her, warm and interested.

"Long. Busy. Exhausting."

"I'm sorry I'm not there. Are you still at the hospital?"

"Just left. I'll be home in about thirty seconds."

"I'll stay on the phone with you until you get upstairs safely."

She grinned. "And then you can tuck me into bed?"

"Something like that." Kyle paused. "I miss you, Laney."

She nodded at the phone, knowing he couldn't see her. Heavy emotion welled up in her chest and she was relieved when her doorman waved her over to the service desk in the lobby. "Hang on a second, Kyle. I have a package." She tucked the phone into the crook of her neck and accepted the small cardboard box. It had a courier delivery label on the front, but no other identifying information. "You still there? I have a mystery box."

"Intriguing." His voice filled with mischief.

It took her a few beats to clue in, but once she did she bounced with excitement. "How did you get my address? And what is it?"

"Your mom was helpful yesterday."

Laney rolled her eyes out of habit, but she was touched by both Kyle's present, whatever it was, and her mother's quiet acceptance of whatever Kyle was. *Your boyfriend, as strange as that might be.* It was the right word, once again, and it felt perfectly right. Her heart pounded in her chest, and she was relieved that Kyle couldn't see her face flush bright red. She swallowed hard as she let herself into her condo.

"Let me just find the scissors...okay, what did you..." her voice trailed off as she pulled the bottles and boxes out of the box. Bubble bath, peppermint foot cream, chamomile tea, chocolate covered espresso beans, and a printed stack of IOU coupons for backrubs. Yeah, he was her boyfriend. Dammit. "Kyle, this is perfect. Oh my god. I'm totally going to have a bath before I crawl into bed. I love this. I love—"

She cut herself off. She squeezed her eyes shut to hold back tears, cursing herself for being suddenly so damn emotional. That empty second felt like a lifetime, but Kyle took over and pulled her back. "I'm glad you like it. I'm sorry I'm not there to run that bath for you. I'd like to wash your hair. And the rest of you." His voice caught on a gruff note and he cleared his throat. "You can give me a detailed report when you wake up, okay?"

"Okay."

"Sleep tight, Laney."

The last thing she did before she drifted off was send Kyle a picture of herself in the bath, surrounded by bubbles.

———

THE WINERY WAS DECKED out for the holidays. Strands of multi-coloured lights lit up a massive fir in the lobby and framed the windows. Glass ornaments filled bowls and mistletoe was hung in every arch. *Ty must be sleeping with a decorator.*

Kyle didn't see his friend in the bustling tasting room, so he cut across the multipurpose great room, currently being set up for the New Year's dance, and made his way to the offices in the loft on the far side of the building. A soft moan, followed by a giggle and papers hitting the floor told him that Ty wasn't alone.

Jesus. He didn't dare interrupt. They probably wouldn't stop. He ducked down the hallway toward Evan's dark office instead. The older West brother was away, but Kyle could use the computer. He wanted to send Laney some MP3s. The songs they danced to the other night. Maybe buy her a Faith Hill album. Anything. Fuck. He just wanted to make her happy again. Keep her constantly happy. Anything to keep her in the mood to take naughty photos, that's for sure.

Her mother had initially been reluctant to get involved, but when Kyle promised that he would only use the information she could provide for good and not evil, and he swore up and down that he wasn't going to be a "weak-kneed, lily-livered, spineless little boy this time around". Claire had made him repeat that one a few times.

She hadn't explicitly asked about his intentions, and he was grateful for that. If she had, he probably wouldn't have been able to make that oath with the same conviction. He was pretty sure that he and Laney were on the same page. His stomach clenched at the caveat. Pretty sure wasn't good enough. But for fuck's sake, neither was nine days. He was doing the best he could under the circumstances.

Down the hall, Ty's office door opened and a stacked blond stumbled out, adjusting her skirt. His friend followed, giving her one last kiss and a pat on the ass. Kyle cleared his throat.

"Hey, man. What brings you here? I thought you were my brother." Ty looked far too pleased with himself as he sauntered into Evan's office and fell into one of the leather chairs under the window.

"Came to see if you needed any help."

Ty waggled his eyebrows.

"With the party, dickhead. For tomorrow."

"Ah, the party. Right. Nope, everything's coming together nicely. It's great to have an events manager now to handle stuff like that." He cracked his knuckles. "To be honest, I wasn't sure you were coming."

Kyle frowned. "Why the hell wouldn't I—goddamn small town—who told you?"

Ty chuckled, then laughed harder again as Kyle's tension grew. "Karen, Ian, Carrie, Evie…take your pick. In the age of smart phones, wildfires have nothing on gossip."

"Fuck me. This isn't anyone's business!" He leapt to his feet, bristling with…something. His muscles were bunching and twitching under skin that felt too hot and too tight. He punched one fist into the other palm. They needed time, which they didn't have, and space, which clearly no one was going to give them.

"Settle, dude. Seriously, what's gotten into you? I've never seen you so wound up over pussy."

Before either of them could process what was happening, Kyle had Ty hauled out of his chair and up against the wall. Kyle's forearm pressed hard into the other man's chest, and Ty opened his mouth but Kyle cut him off.

"She's not…fuck. Don't fucking say that." He eased off. "She went back to Chicago for work."

Ty stared at him like he was an idiot. "So why are you here?"

Maybe he was an idiot, because he didn't understand the question. "To help with the party prep?"

"Not here, numbnuts. Here." He gestured out the window. "In Wardham. Why aren't you in Chicago for the weekend? You don't need to be back at work until what…Tuesday?"

Yeah, he was an idiot of the highest order. He'd thought of visiting her, of course, but in the future. Another stolen week or weekend. Another fling. It hadn't occurred to him to go with her. To be with her. It was only a five hour drive. Why was he thinking about March? He could be in her bed every weekend if she'd have him. *That's a big if.* Dread flooded his guts. Laney had made it clear that she didn't believe he could want her, just her. What if he couldn't break down that wall? Maybe that's why she didn't extend an invitation. *Last time she did that, you broke her heart.*

So what was different now? If anything, he was more entrenched in Wardham than ever before. Laney was right to worry. Every choice he'd ever made had been in favour of his hometown. His friends. His family.

Family. Fuck. The family he wanted had walked out his door in the middle of the night and he'd just stood on the front step and watched. Again.

"Kyle? You done going all alpha male here?" Ty slid along the wall and eased his way back to the chair.

"Not even close. I need a favour."

WHEN LANEY WOKE up hours later, her inbox had a photo of Kyle's hand, gripping the steering wheel so hard his knuckles were white. She giggled, and snapped a quick photo of her bare legs stretched out on the bed. Then another one, this time a close-up of her face.

She hadn't even made it over to her desk before the phone rang.

"Are you trying to kill me?"

"You don't like my pictures?"

"I fucking love your pictures. I just got a hard-on in front of my parents."

Happy laughter bubbled up inside her. "I'm sorry. I mean, not really, but awwwww. I'd have liked to see that."

He growled in her ear. "You want to see it?"

"You wouldn't!" Laney sucked in a breath. "What if you accidentally sent it to your mom? Or your principal?"

"I wasn't talking about a picture, woman."

"Oh. That's a shame, I really would like to see it." That earned her another growl, then her phone chimed with an incoming text message. "How did you do that while we were talking?"

"It's the twenty-first century, sweetheart."

She pulled the phone away from her ear. Kyle's glowering face stared at her, bare need radiating off his digital image.

"You look...hungry. Like a wolf."

"Are you my Little Red Riding Hood?"

She sucked in another breath, and he chuckled. "I think you just might be. Listen, I need to get back inside, but..."

"It's okay. I'll talk to you later." Laney held the phone to her chest for a long while after they hung up.

—————

KYLE RETURNED to the kitchen table and avoided his brother's questioning look as he reached for the mashed potatoes.

"What are you kids doing tomorrow night?" Kyle's parents were going to babysit his niece and nephew so Ian and Carrie could ring in the New Year in style.

"We're going to the winery," Carrie said. "Kyle, do you want drive together? We can share a cab home, then it's just one car to go back and fetch in the morning."

He shifted in his seat. He'd anticipated explaining his absence to Ty, but not his family. He stared at his sister-in-law, willing her to not ask any questions. "Actually, I have other plans."

"Do they involve a smokin' hot doctor?" It would be Ian that would cause problems, of course. Carrie pursed her lips together, holding in a laugh, as her husband turned to explain to his parents. "Kyle's wrapped around the Laney axle again."

Kyle surged to his feet, his cutlery clattering against his plate as his chair skidded out behind him. "You don't know what you're talking about, so shut up."

"Kyle! Little ears, first of all." His father didn't need to raise his voice to make it clear he was displeased. "And second of all, sit your ass down in the chair and don't be disrespecting your mother."

Six year old Kaylie giggled, and shrugged when Carrie gave her the stink eye. "What? Papa said ass. And Uncle Kyle said—"

"We all know what he said. Eat your dinner." Kyle's mother looked down the table. "Kyle, do you want to share something?"

He shrugged. "Not yet."

"Are you going to get hurt over this?" Eleanor Nixon never pulled her punches.

"Maybe. The odds are pretty even, I guess."

"Do you love her?"

Kyle lifted his head and looked his mother in the eye. "I think the first person that should hear those words is Laney, don't you?"

Across the table, Carrie pressed her hand to her chest and smiled. She shared a private look with her mother-in-law, then changed the subject.

17

———

I t had been three days since she'd left Wardham. Probably time to call her mom.

She'd woken Claire and Evie to say goodbye and explain her sudden departure, and left a sticker covered note for Connor and Max. Evie had sent a photo of them making a doctor snowman later that day, but Laney still hadn't talked to anyone at the farm. Her mom knew the drill, and they didn't usually talk more than once a week, but...it wasn't just about being a good daughter, either. Laney hoped that talking to her mom might help her figure out what to do about her mess of unsettled feelings. Yes, it was time to call her mom. *Time to call Kyle as well.* She winced. They hadn't texted or spoken again since last night. He was putting the ball in her court, and she was watching it dribble along the ground.

She tucked that pang of regret away for the moment. She only had a couple of minutes before her hair appointment. Only enough time for a mom, not enough time for a guy.

Claire picked up on the first ring. They exchanged brief updates on the last few days, then Laney dove in. "Kyle sent me a package. He told me he asked you for my address."

"That arrived quickly."

"I don't think he made it himself. It was a gift basket type of thing."

"I hope I did the right thing." Claire's voice ached with worry, and Laney quickly reassured her it was fine.

"We've been texting a bit. I didn't expect him to be so..." A querying silence fell over her, and her mother didn't try to fill in the gaps. "I don't know. Understanding. Supportive. Constant."

"Then what's the problem?"

"I don't know how long it will last." Damn, that hurt to admit. "I can't move home, Mom."

"It's too soon to worry about that." Claire sighed. "I hate to suggest that you just have a fling, but you're a grown up. Just because Kyle lives here doesn't mean he can't make the drive to Chicago. And I'd love it if you visited more, even if your primary reason was a booty call."

Laney laughed. "Oh god, Mom!"

"What? I understand how the world works these days."

The receptionist chose that moment to call her name, and Laney quickly told her mother that she loved her.

As she sat in the salon chair, she closed her eyes and mused. He'd called her twice. All morning she'd thought about calling him, taking the initiative and demonstrating that she was in, committed to whatever this was between them. Sending the photos had been easy. Flirting was easy. Actually making a call was something much more dangerous. An acknowledgement that she cared about him beyond hooking up. With their history, caring was a slippery slope. What could love between them look like? Two homes, five hundred kilometres apart. Two weekends a month, coordinating vacation time, big phone bills and long empty nights.

Not being with him at all, though...the idea of saying goodbye, of pushing Kyle away, caused hot tears to well up behind her eyelids. Blinking furiously, she redirected her attention to the magazine in her lap. The salon wasn't the place to think about breaking up with someone. The other options weren't really options at all. She couldn't move home. And she couldn't ask Kyle to leave Wardham. He'd made it clear that was his happy place, where he'd invested years of teaching service. Where he'd literally started to build his own home. His friends, his family. And it's not like she'd be offering him much. An hour before bed. Half of her weekends.

Isn't that his call, though? Kyle didn't need her protection. He'd drawn that boundary before, he would again if it got to be too much. Stabby pains danced through her gut at that realization. This wasn't completely her decision. He seemed all in, but for how long?

Someone tapped her on the shoulder and guided her over to the wash station. As the highlight foils slipped out of her hair, she bristled at herself. Would she really let it fall apart again?

She needed to go for what she wanted.

Laney pulled out her phone as she left the salon and dialled his number. Fear be damned. He answered on the first ring, his voice eager but breathless.

"Did I catch you at a bad time?" She stepped into the street and hailed a cab. "I'm just heading home, I could call you back when I get there."

"No, it's fine, I was just unloading the truck. I'm glad you called. Are you all ready for tonight?"

"Pretty much. My hair and makeup are done, my introduction notes are written, I've memorized all the key points about donors."

"Do you have your dancing shoes picked out?"

"I don't think I'm going to do much dancing tonight." She flushed as vivid memories of the last dance they shared crashed into her head.

"You love to dance." Kyle lowered his voice. "You should let some fat cats twirl you around the dance floor and make you feel beautiful."

"You wouldn't be jealous?"

He laughed. "Are you kidding me? But at the end of the night, you'd call me. They get you for a moment. You're mine for..."

"For what?" Laney whispered. It was time for the hesitation to end. "I'm yours. Right? I'm yours for..."

Kyle cleared his throat. "Are you almost home?"

She nodded, then remembered he couldn't see her. "Yeah. One more block."

He didn't say anything, and into the silence she spilled all sorts of possible meaning. She took a deep breath and pressed her hand against her stomach. "Kyle..."

"Shhh, it's okay."

"What is that, your new catch phrase? Hang on, I just need to pay the cab." She reached into her purse and grabbed a twenty. She didn't bother to wait for change. It was New Year's Eve, after all. And she had a phone conversation to get back to.

She exchanged nods with the doorman as she walked toward the building. "Please, Kyle. This is really hard for me. I don't know why I'm so scared, I just am."

"You don't need to be scared, beautiful. Look up." She heard the words through the phone and in front of her at the same time. Kyle was standing in her lobby, looking nervous and handsome and oh so very real. He wore a black suit jacket over jeans and a dress shirt, and he was clean shaven. She squeaked as her phone tumbled to the ground and she flung herself into his arms, driving him back a few steps.

"You're mine forever, sweetheart. Forever." Kyle eased her back to the ground and cupped her face in his hands. "I love you so much, Laney Calhoun. I love you here, in Chicago. I love you at the end of a 24 hour shift. I love you in this giant glass building that doesn't seem to have parking for pickup trucks, and I love you even though you don't think you have time or space in your life for a relationship."

"I was wrong." She hiccupped. "I'll make time."

He kissed her, pressing his lips against hers with sweet determination, promising her that it didn't matter because he loved her just the way she was. Her knees buckled, and he eased her against him, his arms sliding solidly around her body. "Can we go upstairs?"

She nodded, and he pulled her tight into his side after she rescued her phone. With his other hand, he grabbed a suitcase that he'd left against the wall. In the elevator, they stood pressed against each other, hearts pounding in anticipation. A tremor wracked Laney's body when they reached her floor. She pressed her key into Kyle's hand and pointed to her door. If she didn't sit down soon, she was going to pass out, and she really didn't want to miss what she was hoping would come next.

Kyle let his suitcase tumble to the ground as the door swung shut behind them. His attention was fixed solely on her, his gaze stripping her naked, not just her clothes, but grabbing her fears, questions and hesitations, flinging them aside as well. She pressed herself against him, still not quite believing that he was there in front of her.

"How attached are you to that pretty hair do?" Kyle murmured against her neck as his fingers made quick work of her buttons.

"Couldn't care less," Laney breathed, shoving his jacket down his arms. "You look nice, by the way."

"I shaved."

"I noticed."

"I love you." Kyle wrenched open her jeans and she wiggled out of them while she worked on his belt buckle and fly.

"Yeah? Because I love you." Her breath hitched as he gripped her hips, his fingers curling under her ass, and then she was jerked up against his chest and he was pressing her against the wall. Her bare legs wrapped around his waist and she rocked her core against his erection.

"Jesus, hang on a second." He fumbled between them, and she realized he was still wearing his jeans. And he was shaking. That made two of them.

"Wait, wait, wait. Let's go into the bedroom." She slid down the wall, her toes reaching for the floor. His hands raked up her sides, like he was searching for a solid handhold.

Any part of me. I won't let you go.

His breath was loud and rough. His hands reached her shoulders, squeezed, then slammed onto the wall on either side of her. Pressing their foreheads together, he took a deep breath and nodded. She captured his lips with hers. "I love you, Kyle. I have no idea how we're going to work this out, but my heart? It's yours." She tugged on his arms, pulling his hands to her body. "My body is yours." She worked on the buttons of her shirt. "Here, touch me."

He helped her lose the shirt, then divested himself of his clothes as well. Standing in the hallway, her in her bra and panties, him in his boxer briefs, they stared at each other. Both breathing hard. Brave and scared at the same time. Kyle skimmed his hands over her shoulders, down her arms, tracing her shape. She shivered, and he picked her up again, holding her high on his waist. She looked down at him with a tremulous smile.

"No more doubt," she whispered. "No more fear."

"Which way to our bed?"

"Turn right. Second door."

He strode down the hall, effortlessly holding her against him, one palm on her ass, the other between her shoulder blades. Shouldering the door open, he found what he was looking for and lowered her gently. "Next time I'm going to fuck you up against the wall. When I'm not such an emotional pansy." He slid her bra straps down her arms, freeing her nipples. "God, I love these." He lowered his mouth, and his next words were muffled.

"Say it again."

He let her breast pop out of his mouth and moved up, covering her completely with his weight. "I love you. You are my everything."

Laney whimpered. "There's so much to talk about still."

"Nothing else matters but waking up next to you and being able to rub your feet when you're tired." He nipped at her lower lip, then sank his mouth into hers for a deeper kiss. Good lord, the man could kiss. She made another helpless noise, and he pulled away. "I'm here. I'm going to have to come and go, but I'm here."

Before she could question all the logistics of what that meant, he flipped over and pulled her on top of him. She lost the bra, and he cupped her mounds together as she started to slowly rock herself toward a first climax. Two layers of fabric separated them, but Kyle wasn't sure she wouldn't drag him with her. He dragged the scrap of silk down her hips, and she stood up to remove them all the way. He shucked his own boxers, and then she sank down, bringing them together.

They moved as one, slow at first, then with more urgency as they climbed toward release. He felt her climax build, felt her flutter around him, and it hastened his own need. He reached between them to tease her clit, and she responded by crying out his name. That did it. His name spilling from her lips and he slammed home, hoping to hell he'd gotten her there.

As the dull roar faded, he realized two things. One, Laney was boneless and blissed out on top of him. Good. And two, he was still hard. He flexed his cock inside her, and she gasped. "Again?"

He nodded and rolled again, pinning her beneath him, alternating tender kisses and hard thrusts. He covered her entire body with his, filling her up with passion and fire, promising companionship, adventure, understanding, support and adoration.

18

___

As soon as she heard the knock at the door later that evening, Laney realized she'd forgotten to make an important phone call.

"Are you expecting someone?" Kyle asked from the bedroom. She bit her lip and pulled on a robe. "Laney? Do you want me to get the door?"

She stepped into view and winced. "There's something that I forgot to mention."

He laid Ty's tuxedo jacket on the bed, crossed his arms and raised one eyebrow. "Oh?"

She licked her lips. This wasn't that big a deal. "That—" the knock sounded again "—is my date for the evening."

Without a word, Kyle turned and stalked to the front door. She hurried after him, admiring his long legs and tight ass in his black suit pants. *Not the time, Calhoun.* Even though she knew he didn't have anything to be jealous over, this was crappy timing. Kyle grabbed the handle and swung the door open just as Rick raised his hand to knock for a third time.

"About time, Laney, leaving a cripple—Oh!" The two men sized each other up. One half-dressed and in her home. The other… "Hi. Rick Masters. I, uh, thought I was taking Laney to the gala tonight."

She bobbed her head around Kyle's shoulder. "Hey Rick. I'm sorry, I should have called. This is Kyle."

"Her boyfriend." For good measure, *her boyfriend* flexed his broad shoulders and she pushed back the instinct to roll her eyes. "I'll be escorting Laney tonight. I'm sorry for the inconvenience."

———

KYLE WASN'T ACTUALLY SORRY, but it wasn't this shmuck's fault that plans had changed. Shit happens. He made room for Laney to step forward to stand even with him. As much as he wanted to close the door and get back to watching her dress, this was her guest to deal with. He harnessed his inner caveman and deferred to her with a nod. She shot him a quick look that told him it was all a bit belated and he shrugged. Again, shit happens.

"Rick, would you mind heading on without me? We'll see you there, I'm sure." Laney smiled sweetly, and the guy on crutches nodded. "I'm sorry about this, I should have called. It just slipped my mind."

"Of course." He shot a quick glance at Kyle, then opened his mouth as if he was going to ask a question. Thinking better of it, he nodded again and turned to the elevator.

Laney turned and glided to her bedroom faster than Kyle would have thought possible. He made sure the front door closed firmly before following.

"You want to tell me what that was all about?" He filled the en suite bathroom doorway, his stance wide, his arms crossed again. She glanced at him for a moment before she resumed applying her makeup in the mirror. "When did you make this date with that guy?"

"Settle down. It's not what you think. We're colleagues, and Rick has escorted me to many of these events. He knew that tonight was just sharing a car."

"So you haven't had sex with him?"

Laney's cheeks flushed pink, but the way her nostrils flared told him it wasn't out of embarrassment. "We weren't going to have sex tonight, and that's what should matter to you." She took a deep breath. "We used to...have a casual understanding. It ended before I went home for Christmas."

His turn for nostril flaring. He couldn't help it.

She sighed and softened her tone. "It was never like what we have."

Kyle pressed his lips together. That wasn't what he had wanted to hear, but she was right. The past didn't matter. He took a deep breath and apologized for being a lunkhead. She flashed a ready smile and he relaxed against the door frame. She put the finishing touches on her face and turned toward him. She glowed. The professional hair and makeup she'd had done earlier were nice, but this was his Laney. Her hair was down, shiny golden waves spilling over her shoulders, and her makeup just accented her natural colouring.

"You are the most beautiful woman in the world," he said huskily, and her wide eyes and parted lips told him his earlier alpha male display was forgotten. Or at least forgiven. "Can I help you get into your dress?"

"Will it actually make it on?" she teased, moving toward her closet. A pale pink satin gown hung on the closet door, but she dropped her robe and stepped past it, searching inside.

Kyle sucked in a breath at the glimpse of her long bare legs topped by barely there nude-coloured lace boy shorts. "Maybe not."

"I was going to wear that pink dress, but now I'm thinking this one might be more appropriate." Laney drifted into view, holding a mass of red tulle to her chest. "It doesn't have a hood, but..."

Kyle stepped back, not trusting himself to be within touching range. He cleared his throat and gestured for her to put it on. She turned her back to him, and his eyes devoured her heart shaped ass as it bobbed around in front of him. She smoothed out the tulle, and finding the centre of the dress, stepped in. Once she had the bodice up and around her chest, she looked over her shoulder.

"Mr. Wolf, do you think you could zip me up?"

"Only if you come closer, little one." His cock strained at the fly of his tuxedo pants, and he thought about telling her to put on the pink dress instead. He wouldn't make it through the night playing nice. She backed up, her eyes locked on his, and he reached forward. He grasped the zipper tag between his thumb and middle finger, letting his index finger blaze a trail up her spine as he inched the dress together, covering her delectable spine at a painfully slow pace.

After doing up the hook and eye just under her shoulder blades, he slid his hands to her hips and turned her around. She looked like an ethereal fairy, her skirt made up of a number of layers of floaty red tulle, her snug bodice covered in the same material. "We'd better go before I bite you."

Her eyes flared bright at the suggestion, and he pulled her into the cradle of his hips. His chest was hot with excitement, like he just might rip his suit open and discover he was Superman. Laney did that to him, made him feel invincible. A quick glance at his watch reminded him that the love of his life had an important public event to get to, and he guided them to the door. She stepped into black pumps, grabbed her wrap and handbag, and they were off.

Tension zinged between them all night. The gala was in a modern event facility in the West Loop, and the glass and white decor was enhanced by a curtain of white lights along the far wall and large black and white photographs of staff and patients from the hospital hanging on the wall like precious art. Everyone that Kyle met raved about Laney's dedication to her patients and her willingness to support the fundraising efforts. He learned about the extraordinary costs that families face when they have a child in the hospital for an extended period of time, and he understood why Laney couldn't leave this community behind. He had accepted that as a fact before, but now it truly made sense.

Shortly before midnight he left her in deep discussion with a donor and went in search of something with which to toast the new year. Waiters were circulating with trays of champagne flutes, but they were being snapped up quickly. He managed to snag two glasses on the far side of the room and turned to find Laney again.

"So, you're her...boyfriend." Rick swung into view.

Kyle nodded, and took a sip of champagne.

"I didn't think Laney did boyfriends."

Kyle didn't owe this guy any explanations, and he didn't want to say anything that she might object to, but he couldn't help but want to clearly stake his claim. "It's a recent philosophical change, I believe."

"How'd you meet?"

"We went to elementary school together." He had first noticed Laney, really noticed her, at a school-wide cross country run when she was in grade six and he was in grade seven. She'd kicked his ass, and he felt the first pangs of pre-teen lust as her long blond ponytail waved back and forth in front of him as she pulled away toward the finish line. He could still remember that she had been wearing a yellow t-shirt and tight black running shorts. She became a part of his life that day, imprinted on him so he was always aware of her presence. On the schoolyard. At the beach. At bush bonfires. As she got older, he wound tight at the thought of her hooking up with someone else, but something held him back. He loved her from afar for ten years before she kissed him. And he had been so damn nervous, his palms sweaty, legs shaking. Fear. He had been riddled with fear, even once they started dating. Fear is what made him push her away at the end of that summer. It kept him from happiness for another twelve years. He had been searching for someone to fit into his life. He felt like an asshole for not realizing until he was thirty-four that his life was wherever Laney needed to be. "I'm moving to Chicago in the summer."

"TONIGHT WAS A BIG SUCCESS."

"Mmmm." She leaned into Kyle's chest and closed her eyes. It was a short cab ride to her condo, but she wouldn't last that long. "I'm so sleepy."

"Then head to Grandma's house," he whispered. "You can crawl into the bed there, I'm sure it's safe."

She shivered against him. Her eyes didn't open, but her hand sought out his erection and palmed it leisurely. His fingers circled her bare shoulder under her wrap. The anticipation had been building all night. She had considered dragging him into one of the conference rooms on the upper level of the event space that she had seen at a planning meeting, but the professional Laney had won that battle. Getting caught having sex by a colleague, or worse, a donor, would have ruined the night.

But now they were alone.

"My, what big hands you have," she whispered.

"That's not my hand," he muttered, gripping her shoulder.

She giggled. "And what big teeth you have."

"The better to bite you with, my dear."

"Better be a promise," she breathed, pressing closer.

He leaned in as if to kiss her, then ducked his head lower, running his mouth down her neck, nipping all the hot spots.

"Come closer, little one." His mouth was higher again, at her ear, and then it was his tongue that she felt, just the tip, tracing the outside edge of her cartilage.

She closed the last few gaps between their bodies, plastering herself against him just in time for the cab to come to a stop in front of her building. Kyle pulled cash out of his pocket and shoved her out the door.

"Hey!" She protested, but she too felt the urgency. His arm was a steel band around her waist as he propelled her onto the elevator, where he made short work of finding her underwear and ripping them out from under her dress.

"Mr. Wolf," she panted. "I don't think that my grandmother would approve."

He growled and slid two fingers inside her, the palm of his hand rocking back and forth over her clit. She lifted one leg, wrapping it around his rock hard thigh, giving him deeper access.

"You've got fifteen seconds to come on my hand, sweetheart," he muttered. His erection pressed into the soft skin at the top of her standing leg, a few centimeters from her hot, wet core, and with each crooked pass of his fingertips over her g-spot, she could feel him swell a bit more.

"I want you inside me," she moaned, her hips swaying to pull their cores together.

He pressed her harder against the elevator wall, and slid his fingers out of her pussy. One finger trailed a lazy circle around her clit, and she felt the clenching start before he spoke again.

"Come for me," he said, his voice low and tight. "Let me feel you coat my hand."

He swirled around her clit once more, and as the elevator doors opened, she spasmed hard, her entire body jerking against him, and as her thighs slid together, trapping his hand, he got the flood of wetness he wanted.

The reality of what they'd just done crashed around her as she took her first uncomfortable step toward her front door.

Kyle slid his arm around her, rubbing circles on her side. "You okay?"

"We just...in the elevator. What if someone else got on?"

He pressed her up against her front door. "No one did. If they had, I'd have dropped your leg and it would have looked like we were just kissing. It's New Year's Eve, it's allowed."

"Oh my god. I think there are security cameras. Oh god." She sank back against the wall.

Kyle chuckled and eased her forward toward the kitchen. "Come on, Little Red Riding Hood. Let's get you a glass of water."

Laney humphed and stomped ahead of him. "It's not funny.

You aren't actually the Big Bad Wolf. You're the level-headed one, what were you thinking?"

He washed his hands, then poured her a glass of water. She was parched, and her heart was still pounding. And he stood there, calm, and still clearly turned on.

"I was thinking that it would be fun to finger you in the elevator." He pulled her against him, and unzipped her dress. "Since I overheard the security guards talking about how the video camera system is being upgraded next week, I knew there's no recording happening over the holiday."

Relief washed over her. "You...you...you are in fact the Big Bad Wolf."

He smiled, clearly pleased with himself. "I try. And it was good, yes?"

She swallowed hard and nodded.

"Good. Then what were you saying about things being big?"

She raised her arms, letting her dress fall to the floor. "I don't remember, but I can tell that you aren't my grandmother."

———

LANEY TURNED and ran for the bedroom. Kyle got tangled up in the puffy ball of tulle at his feet for a second, and by the time he got there, she was sliding backward onto the bed. He stripped off his jacket.

"Say it."

"My, what long arms you have," she whispered.

He unbuttoned his shirt. "The better to hold you with."

"And, uhm. What big eyes you have."

"The better to see you with." He dropped his cufflinks on the side table. "Spread your legs for me."

She complied, licking her lips. "And Mr. Wolf, what strong legs you have."

He stepped out of his shoes and socks, then lost his pants. "The better to chase you with."

She paused, and his cock flexed, urging her to finish the game. Her eyes moved back to his face and her lips parted. He shed his boxer briefs and climbed between her legs.

"Oh, yes," she panted. "What a big..."

He reached between them and spread her moisture with the tip of his erection. "Say it."

"What a big cock you have, Mr. Wolf." She whispered the words so faintly he almost didn't hear them.

He sank into her a few inches, then pulled out, causing her to whimper, but then he was deeper again, and on the third press, in to the hilt. He lay his full weight on top of her for a moment, and pressed his mouth to her ear. "The better to make love to you, Laney."

19

"What are you going to do while I'm at work today?"

Kyle watched Laney pull on black dress pants and a pale blue sweater. It was almost spring according to the calendar, but Chicago was in the midst of being walloped with one last blast of winter. One benefit of staying at Laney's condo for the week—no driveway to shovel. "Shopping, then meeting that teacher I told you about for coffee."

She glanced at him, then her watch. They didn't have time to get into this argument again. He thought that she'd be happy he was looking for jobs. He thought wrong. Skepticism rippled across her face, and he resisted the urge to curse.

She seemed content with the routine they had fallen into since Christmas. They were each making the drive once a month, so they had every other weekend together, as well as nightly conversations and more inappropriate text messages than he'd ever imagined possible. It was good, but it could be so much better. And when they weren't together…maybe Laney was busy enough not to miss him, but all that he had enjoyed before now paled in comparison to the 48 hours he got with her every fortnight. Even the January crush of report card prep hadn't filled the void, and the more frequent games nights his friends were organizing to distract him just wound up annoying him.

And on the weekends she visited him, he hated having to share her with her family, which made him an asshole. He couldn't get enough of her, and there was only one solution to that problem. He had to move to Chicago, sooner than later.

Convincing Laney was proving a challenge. He appreciated that she didn't want to rush him, but damn it, why did it feel like she still doubted he was in this relationship one hundred percent?

He stalked out of the bedroom instead of voicing that question. The answer was obvious, and she had to get to work. Asking it would just lead to a fight that he could script himself anyway. He'd proven his selfishness a long time ago, and a few road trips wouldn't change that. Until he actually made the move to Chicago, she would keep a small part of herself locked up in case he broke her heart.

He yanked the tin of coffee and a filter out of the cupboard and jerked the carafe out of the coffee maker hard enough to move the machine a few inches toward the sink. The rush of cold water at the sink almost disguised Laney's approach, but he felt her warmth a second before she pressed her body full against his back and wrapped her arms around his waist. Her mere touch calmed him. Their relationship was still new, for all of their history, and if this was their only speed bump they were doing okay. Real life was bound to be messy. They were going to disagree about life decisions.

"I love you." She breathed the words into his t-shirt and he took another deep breath. "I'm sorry. I hope that the meeting goes well."

He turned. She smiled up at him. Yeah, she loved him. He cupped her face in his hands. "I'm just exploring options."

"I know. I'm excited. But I'm nervous, too." She fluttered her hands around her head, as if warding something off. "It's so much to think about. And I want to focus on you. Just you. Right here, with me, for a week."

"I want more than a week."

She gripped his hands and pulled herself up, silencing him with a quick kiss. "Make coffee, my man. I gotta go."

He grinned. He liked the sound of that. Her man. Yes, he was. And would be forever. But the logistics of making that happen mattered, and if Laney didn't want to think about the details, he'd take it all on himself.

———

SHE OPENED the door to a bouquet of delicious aromas. Sautéed onion and garlic, sweet sausage, and apples and cinnamon. "Honey, I'm home!" She made the appropriate noises of appreciation on her way past the kitchen to dump her bag at her desk, then padded into her closet to change into comfy clothes.

"What's your poison?" Kyle appeared in the bedroom doorway holding an oversized goblet of red wine and a bottle of beer.

Laney grinned, took the wine glass with both hands and tipped it to her mouth. "Mmmmm. You spoil me."

He leaned in for a kiss, and she shared the taste of the baco noir with him. "And you smile at me, and kiss me like that, and it hardly seems like a fair trade."

"What's for dinner?"

"Sausage, white beans and kale." Her stomach growled, and he chuckled. "I'm glad you approve. And I picked up an apple crisp for dessert, and the second season of The Wire."

He'd introduced her to the show on one of her weekend visits and she was addicted to watching it with him, stretched out on the couch.

"See? Spoiled." She set her wine down on her dresser, wrapped her arms around his neck and licked the triangle of skin exposed by his partially unbuttoned dress shirt. "I'm looking forward to more of this house husband luxury once school is out for the summer."

————

HE SLID his hand into his pocket and rolled the thin platinum band between his index finger and thumb. He couldn't have planned a better segue himself. He drifted a light kiss across her mouth and moved his lips to her ear. "I like the sound of that."

She arched her back, pillowing her breasts against his chest. "Husband?"

"Mmmm. And summer."

"Too bad it'll only be for two months, but—"

"—It doesn't need to be—"

"—it's really for the best that we don't rush anything, right?"

Kyle left the ring in his pocket, and shifted back with a sigh. Now was clearly not the right time. He kissed her again, but this time it was perfunctory, a transition out of the conversation. "Come on, let's eat."

Laney trailed behind him. He could feel confusion radiating off her at his abrupt change in tone, but given how his day had gone, he wasn't sure he'd have the upper hand in that argument —logic and reason weren't on his side. And that was the kicker. It wasn't that Laney didn't want him to live with her. She just wouldn't ask him to give up his career, and apparently, her concern had been well placed. And since she was the smartest person he'd ever met, he was pretty sure that it would only take her another few minutes to figure that out.

"Hey, how was your day?" Apparently not even a few minutes. "I'm sorry, I should have asked first thing."

Instead of answering, he busied himself filling bowls and finding cutlery.

"Kyle?"

He took his time settling their dinner out at the island, then leaned one hip against the counter and crossed his arms. He was disappointed, but it didn't change anything, so there was no reason to overstate the situation. "It turns out that it'll be a challenge to get hired here as an elementary teacher." He tried to wave Laney off as she sucked in a breath and moved toward him, arms outstretched. "Sweetheart, it's fine."

"No, it's not." She squeezed him hard around the middle. "I'm sorry. Again. This is why I didn't want you to rush into moving here. We can do the long distance thing for a while, and I'll see what I can do about maybe organizing a winter locum in Detroit or London. And we'll hire an immigration lawyer."

"No. No more half measures. No more waiting. The back and forth is fine for the short term, but I feel like I'm holding my breath for twelve days at a time. That's not how I want to live my life."

————

LANEY HATED that her mind immediately reminded her she'd heard similar words before. It wasn't the same thing. Kyle wasn't leaving her. He wanted to move to Chicago in a few months like a short-sighted fool in love, didn't he? She was the one putting the brakes on, slowing their relationship down. Had she sent mixed signals?

She'd been dodging this discussion for too long. Time to put on her big girl panties. "Okay, I'm listening. How do you want to live your life?"

"Can we eat dinner first? You're starving." She stomped her foot and he grinned. "Okay, dinner can wait. Let's go sit on the couch."

He tugged her into his lap and squeezed her arm. It felt like reassurance, and she relaxed against his chest. His heartbeat was slow and strong, as always. "First of all, I love you. So fucking much." She smiled into his neck. "I felt that. Laney, I know that I didn't choose you a long time ago, but you gotta know that from now on, there's nothing else that matters to me. First priority for me is spending every night in our bed, every morning making your coffee and every evening sharing dinner with you."

"And what about work?"

He sighed. "Yeah. I love teaching. Love it. Used to think that I lived for it. But it looks like I might need to take a break for a little while."

"So you want to come here and what?" She pushed herself up and turned to straddle him. She had been kidding about the house husband thing, but maybe that could work. "You're social enough, I'm sure you'd find something to do, but…"

"I'm not asking you to support me, Laney. I've got savings." The look on his face was priceless, and she couldn't help but laugh.

"Oh god, no, that's not where I was going! Although that wouldn't be a problem, at all—seriously, you don't think I'd care about that?" He shrugged and she smacked him lightly on the shoulder. "Kyle! What's mine is yours and all that jazz. No, I meant…I don't want you to regret this." *I don't want you to resent me.* "Are you still going to be happy being a house husband a few years down the road?"

"Oh sweetheart, I don't think it's going to come to that." He laughed and stroked her cheek. "As much as I would love to be at your beck and call, I've got a new plan."

"But I thought you said that it would be difficult to get hired."

He nodded. "That's why I'm going back to school." He wiggled his hand under her thigh and pulled something from his pocket. "After my meeting, I dropped in at the university. Turns out they have a pretty decent Faculty of Education."

Something bright sparked in her chest and she sat a little straighter. "And—"

"And the admissions officer thought I'd probably be a good fit for their M.Sc. program."

She squealed and flung herself on top of him. "That's brilliant. Totally perfect. I can't believe I didn't think of that—you are going to be the hottest grad student on campus. I'm going to buy you a backpack."

He chuckled into her hair. "I already have a backpack."

"This one's going to have *Laney's Boyfriend* embroidered on it so all the coeds know to keep their mitts off of you."

He hugged her tight, then eased her off his lap.

She moved back toward their dinner, but turned when she realized he wasn't following. It took her a second to process why he was kneeling in the space between the couch and the coffee table.

"Kyle?" She breathed his name, her voice filled with hope and longing, and she didn't care because even though she should have gotten it before, even though he'd shown her in deed and told her in word, now she really knew that this was forever. And she didn't care about being a cliché, not one little bit.

"Laney." In contrast, his voice was rich and deep, loaded with confidence. But there was hope too, they shared that, and hearing all of that in just her name, the tears started. "Oh sweetheart, if you cry, you're not going to hear the good part."

"It's all pretty good," she whispered, stepping closer to take his outstretched hand.

"Delaney Calhoun, I've loved you since the seventh grade. I'm an idiot, so I didn't realize it until I was twenty-two, and then I let you go, a bonehead move that I will always regret. You went on an amazing journey, and I'm sorry that I wasn't there to support you. You didn't need it, of course, but damn...I wish I hadn't missed it. I don't want to miss anything else. I want to be your rock. Your forever. You're already mine. So I'm here now, on bended knee, asking you to be my wife."

She was nodding before the ring magically appeared in his other hand, and he grinned as big fat tears fell on the sparkling solitaire.

"Will you marry me, Laney?"

The nodding and crying continued as she sank to her knees and he wrapped himself around her. "Is that a yes?"

"Yes! Oh my god, yes." She kissed him hard on the mouth, then pulled back and bit her lip. "The backpack label will have to change."

He sat back on his knees and she climbed on top of him again. Dinner was going to have to wait a bit longer.

EPILOGUE

Cars lined the road between Evening Lane Farm and the school house, and probably stretched just as far again on the other side.

"How many people do you think are over there?" Laney peeked out the window, looking toward her mother's house.

Kyle came up behind her and wrapped his arms around her waist. "Too many. Let's stay here and get naked instead."

"It's our engagement party. Our absence would probably be noticed."

"It'll go all night. We've got some time." He nuzzled her neck and she turned in the circle of his arms. "We're packing, it's a decent excuse."

Most of his clothes were already in Chicago. The furniture was all staying. They were keeping the school house so they'd have a private place to stay when visiting. "No one will believe it. You don't have that much stuff."

Claire and Eleanor had wanted to throw a huge party right after they got engaged, but since Kyle and Laney only had two weekends together each month, their mothers agreed to wait until the summer. Evening Lane was the obvious location. The boat was moved out of the barn to make room for a potluck lunch, and it seemed like everyone in the county had been invited.

They decided to walk over, as the closest parking spot was their own driveway, and a shiny black sports car had just blocked in Kyle's pickup truck anyway.

"You made it, you bastard! I thought you were in France." Kyle stepped forward and clapped Ty on the shoulder as they shook hands.

"Wouldn't miss your engagement party, man. This is a big deal." Their driveway interloper turned and flashed a brilliant smile in her direction. "Laney Calhoun, it's been a long time. Congratulations."

She returned the smile. "Thank you. I hear business is booming. Nice ride."

He clapped his hands together and hooted. "Ain't she, though? Just picked her up yesterday. A little bonus for selling out our subscription this year."

The men talked shop on the walk up the road, and Laney listened with one ear. But the rest of her attention drifted to her surroundings, this place of big skies, dusty roads, fields filled with tall stalks of corn and endless rows of soybeans. There were probably two hundred people ahead at the farm, and she could hear them, but she could also hear the scuff of her boot against gravel, the hearty laughs of her fiancé and then right in front of her, a white butterfly fluttered by and she would swear she heard its wings.

Wardham would always be the home in her heart. But her heart had found a home in the man ahead of her, and with the dog loping along at his feet. As if he knew she was thinking about him, Buddy turned as if to tell her to hurry up, and she laughed quietly to herself. Her life before had been good. Nice. Pleasant. But now...it was so much better. It was real and sweet and complicated and precious.

Kyle entwined his fingers into hers as they arrived at the farm. Ted climbed on top of the picnic table and clinked his beer bottle with his keys. Everyone else joined in, making noise with whatever they had in their hands, and Kyle swept Laney into a kiss that would normally make church ladies blush, but today was greeted with cheers. He raised his hand, and the crowd quieted.

"Thank you all, so much. It means a lot to Laney and me that everyone is so happy about our engagement."

"When's the wedding?" someone catcalled from the back of the crowd.

Kyle laughed and shook his head. "I'm trying to convince my bride to run away with me to Jamaica for that. If our mothers have anything to say about it, I'm sure it will be right here, next summer."

A few people murmured about hurrying up, and Laney stiffened. She didn't want to get into twenty questions about when they were going to have children. Kyle stroked her back and smiled. "There's no hurry, folks. I'm really enjoying being engaged to this beautiful woman, finally—" cheers sounded loudly to that pronouncement "—and when we exchange vows, it'll be when it's right for us."

Claire was the first to hug the bride-to-be, which started a chain reaction that suspiciously resembled a receiving line. An hour later, Laney had talked to almost everyone there. A few people tucked envelopes of money into her pocket, which she found quite touching, and no one asked the baby question.

She made her way to the barn, her stomach growling. She'd seen people walking around with plates of Mrs. Frid's secret meatballs, and she hoped there were some left. Ted was there, along with a handsome young man.

"Laney, have you met Liam yet?" She'd just forked a meatball into her mouth, so she shook her head. "My sister's boy. He's come to stay with me for the summer. He's looking to buy property here."

Liam shook his head and laughed. "Uncle Ted, you gotta stop introducing me as a boy."

She chuckled and accepted his outstretched hand. "Nice to

meet you."

"Congratulations. I've heard a lot about you, and your family."

"Thanks. Have you met my mom and my sister yet? They're both around..." Laney swiveled her head in vain. "They're somewhere. What kind of property are you looking for?"

"I'm not sure. I'll know when I see it. Maybe a duplex, something I could fix up and rent out."

She felt Kyle approach before he spoke. "Hey, you must be Ted's nephew."

"Word travels fast, eh?" Liam nodded.

"Mr. Wilson told me that the young newcomer was hitting on my woman."

Laney smacked Kyle lightly on the stomach. "I told you not to call me that in public."

He growled in her ear, and she grinned at the other two men. "Excuse me, gentlemen, I need to have a word with my fiancé." She laid a quick kiss on Kyle's jaw. "But first, I need to eat something."

They loaded up plates of food and settled on straw bales just outside the barn.

"This is overwhelming," Laney said, taking in the celebration. "There's a lot of love in this town."

"There's a lot of love on this straw bale too," Kyle murmured.

"I'm being serious." He shot her a look that said, *So am I.* She didn't doubt it for a second. He'd proven his love for her many times over the last few months, even though he didn't need to. "Aren't you going to miss this place, though?"

He took a long, slow drink of beer. She appreciated that he didn't blow off the question. It's not like Chicago had ever been his dream. He was leaving almost all of his life goals behind when they headed out tomorrow.

"If we never came back again, then I'd miss it. If this was the last Wardham potluck for me, I'd be sad. But we'll be back for holidays and the odd vacation."

"Not every vacation?"

He shook his head. "No. I'm being serious now too, Laney. Our next vacation isn't going to be shared with our family, or spent driving between Chicago and Wardham. You want to know what I'm excited about?" Her breath caught in her throat. She did, she really did. He took another sip of beer and gave her a smoldering look. "You. A string bikini. A private beach."

She bit her lip. "That sounds perfect."

"I'm telling you, sweetheart...Jamaica. Or Hawaii. I'm not picky. We don't need to tell them." He nodded toward their mothers. "Let them plan a big party. Let's just go away and get married, just the two of us."

He slid his lips across hers and she nodded. His plans were always the best.

THE END

Keep reading Where Their Hearts Collide (Karen & Paul) and When They Weren't Looking (Evie & Liam) — and later in the series, check out Perfect No Matter What, Laney & Kyle go to Vegas!

I ALSO HAVE a mailing list that I use to give readers a heads-up about new releases and big sales. If you sign up, you'll also be given an opportunity to read new releases before they hit stores!

subscribe to my newsletter!

- DEALS
- HOT NAVY SEALS
- QUARTERLY KINDLE GIVEAWAYS
- BE THE FIRST TO HEAR ABOUT
ALL NEW RELEASES!

—Zoe

ACKNOWLEDGEMENTS

AKA THE PEOPLE WHO ROCK MY WORLD

THERE'S a long list of people I need to thank.

My husband, who didn't even blink when I said I wanted to write a romance novel. Or when I wasn't even finished this one and I told him that it was going to be a series, and I'd plotted out the next four books. I'd say I was sorry for typing my way through all those episodes of Castle and New Girl, but we both know I'd be lying. Thank you. I love you muchly.

Rachel, who was the very first person to read Laney & Kyle's story. I will never forget the thrill of reading your email.

Lori, who cried in McDonald's when she finished the inserted chapter. You were my first fan, and that means the world to me.

Andraena, who asked if she could add the book on Goodreads. Yes, now you can! And holy crap, isn't that cool?

Natalie, who has heard more random plot meanderings than anyone else, and has always been up for those conversations, even when they didn't really go anywhere.

My mother-in-law, because she caught a bunch of typos, and sorted me out on the teaching details. Any mistakes that remain are my fault, not hers. In the same breath, I need to thank my father-in-law, for picking up my kids from school, making me dinner, and listening to me yammer on about anything and everything.

My sister, who has talked about the business of publishing with me more than anyone else. Thank you for your patience!

Hannah, another early confidant, who took yet another career turn idea totally in stride. You are a steadfast friend.

Nadia, Shandy and April, who all took a turn at beta reading. Thank you for your feedback, it helped make this book better.

Cora and Molly. I wasn't sure about the idea of critique partners until I found you. Now I get it. Thank you for pointing out where I said the same thing in triplicate, misused big words, skipped little words, and made up my own rules for punctuation. Thank you for reading my long ass emails about the series arc, business plans, and the occasional crisis of confidence.

People on the internet! More awesome folks than I ever expected.

Twitter friends, especially those who did #1k1hr challenges with me across January and February, and anyone who talks about being a feminist romance writer.

The amazing members of the kboards, Absolute Write and Romance Diva forums, who are an astounding wealth of publishing knowledge, but most of all, are passionate cheerleaders for the art of writing.

The women of TB, without whom I wouldn't have thought to search for an online writing forum in the first place.

And finally, my readers. Everyone who has bought this book, joined my mailing list, written a review, tweeted or blogged or posted on Facebook...I can't thank you enough for your support. I love to hear from you!

ABOUT THE AUTHOR

Zoe York lives in London, Ontario with her young family. She's currently chugging Americanos, wiping sticky fingers, and dreaming of heroes in and out of uniform.

Connect with Zoe:
www.zoeyork.com
zoeyorkwrites@gmail.com